PIP AND THE TWILIGHT SEEKERS

To read more about Pip and friends,
look out for all the **Spindlewood** books:

Pip and the Wood Witch Curse

Pip and the Twilight Seekers

Pip and the Lost Children

And meet Stanley Buggles in the
Something Wickedly Weird books:

The Werewolf and the Ibis

The Ice Pirates

The Buccaneer's Bones

The Curse of the Wolf

The Smugglers' Secret

The Golden Labyrinth

Visit Chris Mould at his website:

www.chrismouldink.com

PIP AND THE TWILIGHT SEEKERS

CHRIS MOULD

Hodder Children's Books

A division of Hachette Children's Books

First published in Great Britain in 2011
by Hodder Children's Books

1

A Catalogue record for this book is available from the British Library

ISBN 978 0 340 97070 6

Printed and bound in the UK by
CPI Bookmarque Ltd, Croydon, CR0 4TD

The paper and board used in this paperback by
Hodder Children's Books are natural recyclable
products made from wood grown in
sustainable forests. The manufacturing
processes conform to the environmental
regulations of the country of origin.

Hodder Children's Books
A division of Hachette Children's Books
338 Euston Road, London NW1 3BH
An Hachette UK company
www.hachette.co.uk

WHICH EXPLAINS THAT WHEN THE BLIZZARD STOPPED, THE BEDLAM WOULD BEGIN

The winters are long, here in the Hollow. Cold and thick and deep. Snowstorms sweep across the valley and through the city, tearing through the streets between the houses and piling drifts up against the doorways, whistling between the trees and lacing thick frost around the trunks and branches.

The clawed hands and spindly claws of the forest creatures had retreated into the barky holes of the Spindlewood trees. The thick white of the forest floor was free of their cloven hoof marks and lumbering footprints. Even Jarvis, the city warden, sat cooped up in his hovel, unable to venture out in search of strays. He hated children and he would stop at nothing to be rid of them. But right now, his carriage lay broken upon the ground, its axle crushed, the loose wheel discarded and covered in snow.

No one had moved for some time. Not since those three children had escaped the evils of the forest by the skin of their teeth and had Jarvis and the rest of the woodsfolk screaming after them.

But now the wind stopped. The hurling of snow and chilled air came to an abrupt halt. Beneath the deep drifts were shattered roof tiles and broken chimney pots. Fractured branches from nearby trees poked out like spring buds. But this was no growing season. The freezing winter was still waging war against the world.

'Crank up the fire, Esther,' urged Jarvis, as he sat

lazily huddled up to the fireplace with one hand and one hook tucked into his armpits. He watched, amused, as the crow pulled meagre twigs from the basket and nosed them into place, dancing around the spits of crackling orange.

Eventually he rose from his chair and hooked back the drab, rotted curtain that framed his frosty window. He breathed on the glass and circled his hand on the pane. 'The blizzard has stopped, Esther. It's time to seek out our revenge and lay our hands on those pesky little city rats. We know they're here. I always get my prize in the end,' he said proudly, one eye shut and the other squinting out through the glass, his bulbous nose squashing against the pane.

Jarvis had been tracking his mind back through the recent turmoil in the Hollow. He'd almost had those three children in his grasp. He'd come so close to putting them in the forest keep. But they'd escaped and now he boiled with anger.

All through the blizzards that had followed after the children's escape, he had sat inside and turned things over in his mind. He could still see them. The smallest was a young boy whom he knew to go by the name of Pip. The next, a young girl, memorable by her rats' tails of hair and ragged clothes. But the biggest, a large boy, was somehow more familiar. That tubby-cheeked face kept coming to him. He'd seen it somewhere before and he knew it would come back to him if he thought long and hard enough.

'Time to venture out, I think,' said Jarvis, announcing his next move to Esther.

'But what of the carriage?' begged Esther. 'And the

broken wheel?'

'I'm going to walk to the tavern, Esther. Something is preying on my mind.' Jarvis seemed to be lost in thought.

He was about to step out through the door when he turned back. He wandered over to the hearth and, lifting his left arm, he sharpened the tip of his hook against the stone lintel. He took a long proud look at its pointed end, gave it a shine with the corner of his black cloak, and then wrapped the cloak around himself and disappeared into the night, leaving deep footprints in the thick of the snow.

WHICH TURNS OUR ATTENTIONS TO PIP AND HIS COMPANIONS

Pip had not heard the expression 'lying low' until now. Apparently it meant staying quiet and keeping your head down after having caused a ruckus. And so that's just what was happening at the Deadman's Hand. Frankie, Pip and Toad had been hiding at the tavern while the blizzard blew over the city and all the marks of their escape from the forest were covered over by the snow.

But for how long were they safe at the inn? They didn't know. Sam was on edge. His own son, Toad, was the first of the three children. Sam had harboured him since his birth in the Hollow. The death of Toad's mother had meant that he had done this alone. The second child was the boy Pip. He had arrived, quite by accident in the back of a carriage, in an attempt to escape his own grim circumstances, and not realizing that his escape lead him to something far more dangerous. The third was the young girl, Frankie Duprie, whom they had rescued from the clock tower after her family had tried to escape the authorities. The rest of the Dupries were now thought to be imprisoned in the city keep.

They must tread carefully. Sam had already sent word through the city to the Duprie family that their daughter was safe at the inn. But who knew what might happen to the information along the way if it got into the wrong hands. The authorities would be all over him. And what about the forest people? They had already been riled by the escaping children. He did not want them knocking at his door.

They had been spending their days watching the blizzard while wrapped up cosy and warm by the fire. They'd baked cakes and pies and played games and ran around the building. Toad had shown Pip and Frankie all the secret parts of the old tavern and Sam had read them dark stories through the night when only the embers of the fire were left to light the way. 'Just one more story,' Toad would plead as they sat on the edges of their seats into the early hours. And they would all cheer excitedly when Sam opened the pages again and began to read.

At night they were packed tightly together, their makeshift beds forming a neat line across the hidden annexe. 'I quite like this arrangement,' announced Pip. 'I know it's a tight squeeze but it makes me feel safe.' Then he would tell them his tales of his dreadful days at the orphanage and how he had longed to escape its clutches.

If the truth be known, Pip had not known companionship until now. Despite the grim circumstances of the Hollow, he felt a sense of belonging growing upon him. Sam and Toad were as near to family as he had ever had and he was quickly getting to know Frankie since she had joined the group. There was a hollow space inside him where the fulfilment of family life should be but somehow his new surroundings were helping to heal the wound.

Late one night he awoke to Frankie sobbing. 'What is it?' he whispered.

'I'm frightened, Pip,' she confessed.

'Of what?' he asked. 'The forest and its creatures? And that we may be caught?'

'No, not that, although the forest fills me with dread,' Frankie said. 'I fear for my family. That I might never see them again and that they may come to harm and I might never know.'

Pip didn't know what to say. He knew that those dangers were real. He swallowed a lump in his throat. 'It will be OK,' he whispered and he held out his hand to her. Frankie smiled unseen in the darkness, closing her fingers around his palm, and they fell asleep to the sound of Toad snoring.

Outside there was a change in the air. A stirring in the water. It was unlikely that the peace would last for long. The dying of the blizzard would cause a livening in the forest, and those who sought to upset the quiet of the streets were already awake.

THE BIT BEFORE
CHAPTER THREE

There was a small matter which may at some point prove to be a problem. Somewhere in the Hollow sat Captain Dooley. A harmless-looking figure of an old soldier from the civil war, fashioned from Spindlewood. Of course he looked harmless. How could he not? He's just a plaything, put together by the toymaker, long since gone from the Hollow after the children were outcast. But there was something in his make up that spelled danger. He was a blabbermouth. He spoke of the secrets of the Hollow, and when I say secrets I mean those hidden children. Told anyone who asked, exactly where they were.

And how does a rickety old wooden toy spill secrets? I hear you ask. It would have to be cursed with some kind of evil sorcery. Some wicked spell that only worked because it was crafted from those Spindlewood trees and evil ran through its woody veins. Well, I'm afraid that whole crazy idea of curses and sorcery was quite possible down in Hangman's Hollow. That dark forest was home to all kinds of sinister goings-on.

For long enough he had stayed hidden in the darkness of an old cloth sack in the corner of a disused attic. That was until the sack dropped through the chimney stack and landed in a dusty fireplace. A prying hand had lifted him from the darkness and placed him upon the mantelpiece of the disused river cottage, dusting him down and leaving him there and not knowing that he would only cause trouble.

He was stirring now, thinking hard. The faces of all the children in the Hollow were coming to him. He could see where they hid, a perfect picture forming in his mind. A ripple of excitement made his little wooden body creak and with it, his rounded moon eyes warmed up the dank light, like candles glowing. He felt that quite soon, someone was going to find him. He was ready to say so much. He knew where they all were. It seems quite unimaginable, but if you had been right there you would have sworn that his little wooden mouth opened and that he had managed a few desperate words. It sounded just like: 'Bring out your children. Here comes the Captain.'

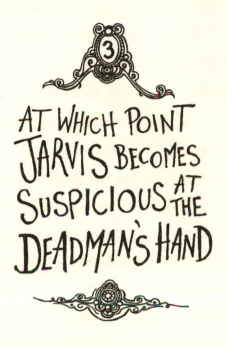

AT WHICH POINT JARVIS BECOMES SUSPICIOUS AT THE DEADMAN'S HAND

The fading of the howling gales had now ensured the Deadman's Hand was brimming with city folk. The fire crackled and local life poured back into the old place. Voices laughed and sang and music filled the air. Tobacco smoke billowed upwards and candles flickered at the tables.

Up above, the children were settled in their hiding

places, keeping themselves amused and out of harm's way. Toad was emptying his bed of crumbs and bits of pastry. Pip lay in his pit, watching, chuckling to himself and shaking his head. Frankie sat quietly with her nose in some old book that she'd found.

Down below, the low rumble of chatter and laughter continued, but silence fell when the hook-handed man stepped inside. He shook his tattered cloak at the door and kicked his boots on the step. With his familiar movement – head down, cloak pulled over the hook – he took his table in the corner.

Sam knew the man's drink and delivered a tankard to the table. Voices returned and the noise level picked up again and things went on as normal.

But this was no ordinary visit to the inn. Something was eating away at Jarvis. Sam was used to his visits and it was not unusual to find him sat at his table in the corner. But the recent turmoil had set the whole place on edge and Sam knew Jarvis would be seeking revenge.

Jarvis was here for a reason. Sure, he liked a drink, but that pesky kid's face had stuck in his mind and he was somehow sure at the back of his mind that the

Deadman's Hand held the answer. He didn't know why or how, but his nose had taken him in the direction of the inn. And Jarvis's nose was never wrong!

Frankie was distracted from her reading by the sound of footsteps. She looked up, her eyes fixed expectantly on the door to the annexe. Feet came carefully up the staircase, moving almost silently along the corridor. The doorway was forced open. It was unusual for Sam to appear in business hours, but he was on double alert.

'He's here. Just make sure you're extra quiet. No movement.' And then he was gone, as quickly as he had entered.

Frankie felt her heart sink. It seemed that they had spent so long protected by the storms and without the threat of Jarvis that to know of his return filled her with fear. The room fell silent for a moment.

The three children stared at each other. 'He'll never find us here,' said Toad. 'We're safe as houses.' And he picked up another cake from his collection and swallowed it whole as he remade his bed.

'That's disgusting!' said Frankie, 'Didn't your father

ever teach you to chew your food?'

'No time for chewing,' insisted Toad. 'If we need to escape quickly, we'll have to pile some food down and get out. Swallowing food is a skill!'

Pip just stared at Toad and then looked at Frankie and again he shook his head in disbelief.

It had only taken a few sips from his ale before Jarvis's mind had clicked into place. He was staring across the room. There it was, looking right at him. He knew he'd seen that kid's face here before. He stood up and crossed the floor. The place went quiet again.

People watched him.

There was an oil sketch of Toad on the wall. It had always been there, amongst the other portraits of the city folk. Mister Sweeney from the foundry, Mrs DeGale and her two youngsters and a large drawing of the Malvern girls, drawn before they'd gone missing. They were reminders to the city folk of their young ones.

'Who is this boy?' questioned Jarvis with the tip of his hooked hand held against the nose of the drawing.

The place went quieter still. There
were those who had no idea and
those that knew Sam and Toad
well. But no man nor
woman from the city
would open their
mouth and betray
the boy.

'Landlord.
Who is this
boy that sits
on your
wall? You must
know him?'
Sam stared.
'Perhaps you
should sit
down and
enjoy your
drink,
Mister
Jarvis,' he

answered, reluctant to betray his own kin. 'You're upsetting my customers.'

'You folks listen good,' Jarvis continued. 'I know you have all got your offspring hiding. My patience has run thin and my bones are tired of searching these frozen streets. I'll flush them out, all of them. You mark my words.'

He took another close look at the boy and then his gaze fell on Sam. Sam panicked that for a moment the resemblance may have caught his eye. Maybe it had. Jarvis drew his shiny hook across the canvas and slit Toad's face from the corner of his eye to the point of his chin. He stormed across the room, sending his tankard flying across the floor, and disappeared into the night.

'It seems to have gone quiet down there all of a sudden,' said Pip, his voice lowering itself into a whisper. Toad stopped in his tracks, cupping a hand over his ear to listen.

'You're right,' said Frankie, closing her book and pricking up her ears. 'Do you think everything is OK?'

There was anxiety in her voice.

'It's fine,' said Toad. 'Everything is fine.' And he climbed the ladder to spy through the scope that was positioned at the drawn curtain, allowing a good view of the city.

'You OK?' said Pip, turning to Frankie.

'Yes,' she answered. 'I'm OK.' But when she lay down in the dark that night she knew that things would not stay the same forever.

Toad never seemed bothered by anything. He could talk for hours on end, he ate like a horse and he made every move at a blistering pace until the moment his head hit the pillow. And then, he snored like a bear and kept everyone else awake.

But Frankie knew when Pip wasn't sleeping. He tossed and turned in his bed and she knew his troubled past was what tied his sheets in knots.

Sometimes she would whisper to him in the dark, 'Are you there, Pip?'

And he would answer 'yes', because he knew that she was asking him if he was awake. And then they'd chat while Toad snored.

'I guess we're your family now, eh, Pip?' Frankie would say.

And he would smile and say that yes, they really were.

'But there's something missing,' he added one night, as he felt himself dozing off into sleep.

'You mean your parents?' quizzed Frankie.

'I don't know,' said Pip. 'I don't know. I just know there's a space inside me where something else should fit.' But the more he thought about it, the more he wasn't sure.

'One day the Hollow will be safe again. Then we'll all feel better,' assured Frankie.

Pip heard her voice but he was too tired now to force a reply. He tried to mutter something, but he felt himself drifting helplessly into slumber.

IN WHICH A SMALL INCIDENT WILL SOON PROVE TO BE DISASTROUS

Now the snow had died it was safe for
Mister and Mrs McCreedy to move into
the riverside cottage. The McCreedys
had worked long and hard to escape
their circumstances and finally
they were ready to move into a
home of their own. They

had more space here for their basket weaving and they would be close to the market square where they plied their trade. Now, while the revellers drank at the inn, they were wheeling their small cart across the city to the new place. Sure, it needed work doing to it. But it was better than the cramped hovel they had previously been in and so they had packed up their things and begun to move.

They wheeled their cart nervously through the streets, knowing that should they be caught in the act, they would suffer at the hands of the authorities. A suspicious Mister Jarvis leaving the tavern was not helpful.

'Mrs McCreedy, you seem to be struggling there. Perhaps I can help.'

Jarvis tipped the cart on to its side and rifled through their belongings.

'No, please, Mister

Jarvis, I can manage, thank you,' Mrs McCreedy insisted, knowing that he was eager to uncover her secret.

'You're lucky this time,' he said. 'But in the end, I'll have them all. I'm not stupid, Mrs McCreedy. I know a maternal woman when I see one. I can see it in your face. As sure as eggs is eggs, you got kiddies hidden away somewhere, I know it.' He grinned.

'Excuse us,' said Mister McCreedy, shoving his weedy frame past Jarvis and picking up the spilled belongings before heading indoors.

'No one likes a mess,' said Mrs McCreedy. 'But at least we have space for our little treasure. You can come out now,' she said. 'We're home and dry.'

And then, like a surprise from a jack-in-a-box, out popped the youngest of the McCreedys, revealing that the bottom of the wheeled cart, now sat in front of the fire, was a false one.

Young Edgar must have been no more than four years old but already he was aware of his status in the Hollow. He knew when to keep his head down and stay quiet.

A pile of discarded rubbish was pulled out from the fireplace. A couple of boxes, a dust-covered sack and a heap of odds and ends. Dry wood took its place in the hearth and a spark of life sent the twigs and branches glowing and blistering. Candles were lit around the parlour and a pan of water was hung over the warming fire.

Edgar climbed up on to the chair and retrieved what had until now been perched on the mantelpiece. An old wooden soldier, smart as could be in his little red coat and shiny black boots. He stared hard at the little fellow until a feeling of horror came over him. The eyes stared back at him and they seemed to hold his gaze until his own eyes watered. They shone like tiny moons and he found that he was unable to let go of the little wooden man.

And then Edgar could have sworn that the soldier spoke his name. 'Master McCreedy, first-born son of the wickerwork man. His mother carries a sibling, yet she doesn't know just yet. Time will tell. Let's hope she is careful, down in the Hollow.'

Edgar stared, unsure about what had just been said.

Then without knowing why, he tucked the Captain into his jerkin. When he finally went to sleep at the end of the day, the small wooden figure sat perched on the end of his bed.

The cellar was dark and dingy. It was no place for a young boy. But there was to be no choice. In the darkness of the room while Edgar slept, the eyes of the wooden soldier still glowed.

AT WHICH POINT WE SUFFER A SMALL INTERRUPTION

Before Frankie's family had been taken by the authorities, they had supplied the inn with bread. For some time now Sam had been struggling by on his own. But since Frankie had arrived she was making her mark on the place and showing him just how it was done.

When Pip and Toad were still sleeping through sunrise Frankie would be up and about in the scullery, mixing the dough and warming up the clay oven. She was not afraid to work and Sam was now used to coming downstairs to the smell of freshly baked bread and the sight of little Frankie covered in flour from head to toe. She would sing quietly to herself in the back kitchen and Sam would watch her sadly, knowing she longed for her family.

A crashing sound came at the door. *Thud, thud, thud.* Angry voices came through the air. Hooves could be heard clattering in the street outside. Sam panicked, and in trying to look and see who was there he neglected to ensure that Frankie was hidden.

The door was being forced, so much so that Sam was coerced into opening it to avoid it being demolished altogether. He was greeted by the stout figure of Hector Stubbs and several other city men on horseback. Stubbs was the city mayor. But others knew him only as a warmonger and a troublemaker. His plan was to capture every hidden child to join his army to wage war on the forest. He was both saviour and enemy to the youth of the Hollow. He longed to triumph over the creatures of the Spindlewood, but the price was too much to pay. City folk would perish alongside their children. Fathers and sons, mothers and daughters. And what did Hector care? He sought only to improve the city.

The city was at war with the forest. Creatures spilled out from the woods at night and filtered into the streets and alleyways. To gain their domination over the city they searched for the children to make prisoners of them. The authorities swept children from the streets to discourage the beasts from entering the city.

This was no place to be growing up. But for those that happened to be there, there was no choice. To be a youngster in this place was a crime. Children were becoming a thing of the past, and those that were there moved through the city after dark. But to do so was to risk being caught by the twilight seekers, the creatures of the forest, or the authorities and the city guardian Mister Jarvis. And though he was supposed to be on the side of the authorities, when it came to double dealing with the forest types, he couldn't help himself.

'Routine check, landlord,' groaned Stubbs. 'We

require to inspect the premises for children. Keeping children hidden is a violation of city laws in the present climate.' And he reeled off some old nonsense that Sam had heard before. He frequently expected their inquisitive visits and he was used to their prying eyes. He kept them at the door as long as he could to make sure that the children were given the chance they needed.

Stubbs stormed through the inn, followed by his men. He showed no mercy, turning tables, pulling out drawers and opening cupboards, and Sam winced at every move for he had no idea what Frankie had done to hide herself. She could be anywhere.

Sam backed into the scullery. Frankie had gone but small footprints could be seen in the flour that lay upon the floor. Quickly he disturbed them with his feet, dispersing the white dust. Where had she gone?

At length, Stubbs and his men gave in. No obvious traces could be seen. They'd peered into the cellar, skirted round the bedrooms and upstairs spaces and even helped themselves to the drink.

When at long last they left, Frankie emerged like a

small ghost from the flour
barrel. She was covered in white
dust.

Sam could only smile with
relief. For now at least, they
would not be subject to further
suspicion.

But not far away, someone else
thought differently. Someone
who couldn't get the image of
Toad out of his mind. He lay in
bed and all he could see was the
Deadman's Hand. The paint
flaking from its sign as it swung,
creaking in the chill wind, and
that drawing on the wall, the one
he had slit from corner to corner.
He would see that face again,
and soon. He was sure of that.

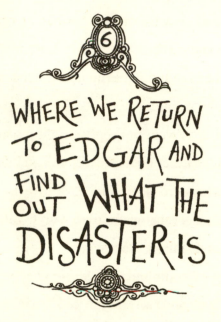

WHERE WE RETURN TO EDGAR AND FIND OUT WHAT THE DISASTER IS

Edgar didn't like the new house. He didn't like his room, nor did he like his bed. He had terrible dreams and he wanted to return to the old place.

'It's the rotten soldier's fault,' insisted Edgar.

'Poor old Mister Soldier,' said Mrs McCreedy. 'You can't blame him. He's just an old wounded hero, sent here to make you feel welcome in your new home.'

'He's evil,' said Edgar and he threw the figure across

the room and watched him land in a folded heap in the corner.

'I'm sure it's quite normal,' explained Ely McCreedy to his wife. 'Edgar has had an ordeal. Moving home can be quite distressing for children. After all, he is in hiding. Who knows what such a thing does to a child!'

When Edgar went to bed that night it was not until the early hours that he finally felt the weight of his eyes reduce him to sleep. But he tossed and turned again and his dreams were filled with nightmare creatures and sinister voices.

He rose from his bed, his eyes opened wide, but all the while he stayed asleep. Pushing back the warmth of his bedclothes he slid into the shoes that were tucked under the frame. And then he walked across the room and picked up the figure of the old wooden soldier, holding it tightly in his hand.

Then, without any hesitation, he walked up the step into the parlour and unlatched the front door. His movements went unheard by his parents and he stepped out into the night. He was now under

the glowing torchlight that
was fixed to the wall of the house.
He marched purposefully across the street
and through the stone archway that lead to
the footbridge.
In a short while he had walked a good way
across the Hollow and now he headed,

unheedingly, into the woods. As he did so Captain Dooley's eyes shone brightly, glowing like little white moons in the snowy crisp darkness of the Hollow, as if to affirm his satisfaction. If that little wooden face of his could have smiled, it would have done so.

'Well, well, well. A little boy lost,' came a voice that seemed to appear from nowhere.

A tall figure loomed over Edgar McCreedy. He had strange white hair, one dark eye, one milky grey eye and two sets of long arms, but the boy seemed not in the least alarmed. Not even the sight of the wolf that walked alongside him was enough to perturb him.

'You let me take care of your little wooden soldier, my boy, and come along with me,' said the man. 'Mister Roach will look after you for sure.'

Edgar handed the figure of Captain Dooley to Roach without so much as a shrug of his shoulders and then he took his hand and off they walked, into the thick of the Spindlewood Forest.

THE BIT BEFORE CHAPTER SEVEN

It was, oh, so cold, but the Captain had a feeling he had not had in a long while, almost as if he was returning home. The fresh cool air, the smell of Spindlewood and the drowsy, dreamy feel of the forest. He opened his eyes to the trees. Endless pillars of frosted white bark that reached out forever, winding and twisting a snakelike walk into a black wilderness. 'There's no place like home,' whispered the Captain quietly to himself, for he knew he should only speak when spoken to.

IN WHICH THE CAPTAIN HAS MUCH TO SAY AND ALL HELL BREAKS LOOSE

Toad had done it again. He'd lain there in the dark telling his sinister tales of the Hollow into the early morning and then suddenly he was asleep and snoring, leaving Pip and Frankie half frightened out of their wits.

'How does he do that?' said Frankie. 'You know, falling asleep like that. Instantly, without any warning!'

Pip chuckled to himself. Good old Toad. Seemingly

nothing bothered him. But Pip did not have quite the same way of dealing with things. His mind turned with the events of the Hollow and his troubled past chased on after him through the dark hours.

He was eager to change the subject.

'What is it like,' he began, 'to be part of a family? You know, brothers and sisters and parents?'

'Oh, don't remind me,' Frankie said. 'I miss them terribly, the young ones especially. I miss all their little ways. How they laugh and sing and make fun and how they're always jolly.'

'And what of your parents?'

'I miss them too. My mother's arms around me and my father's smile. They are good people, Pip. They just want to live in peace. They do no harm.'

'You'll find them again one day,' promised Pip, 'I know you will.' And he felt that he could somehow sense her pain. They lay in silence in their beds, pulling their sheets around themselves to fend off the cold.

Pip's mind wandered as he lay alone in the darkness. Why was he without sisters and brothers? Who were his parents? Perhaps he was part of some wrongdoing in the past and had blanked out the details, something that meant he was not allowed the kind of life he would have loved. He had that feeling again – the one that felt there was a part of him missing. As if a piece of him had been removed and it had left a hole right there in his side. He tossed and turned in his bed and nursed the pain until sleep crept upon him and carried him through the twilight.

The forest was still. Cold and crisp and calm. But as Roach returned with young McCreedy, noises spilled among the trees. Howls and barks and strange hoots that only the forest folk could understand. They escalated in a whirling cacophony of sound, louder and louder. Things gathered and drew close, inspecting at a distance, watching in wonder and wild excitement. Wood witches came near, too near, cackling and cawing with their crows and wolves at their sides.

The boy remained trancelike as they poked and pawed him and inspected him closely.

'A child,' came an excited voice. It was followed

with gasps and 'oohs' and 'ahhhs'.

'Urghhh!' said Stixx. 'Ugly little fella, in't he?'

'Yeah, pig ugly,' said Pugg, her nose wrinkling up in disgust, as her eyes narrowed to an enquiring squint.

And then they saw that Roach carried the old soldier in his hand and the excitement turned to pandemonium. They began to tug at his arms and legs until they almost broke his little wooden limbs. Roach lost his temper and pushed them all away. His wolf companion growled at the onlookers, forcing them backwards into submission.

A crow landed on a nearby branch ahead of her master, who followed on quickly.

'Esther,' said Hogwick. 'Where is he?'

'He's here.'

And then, predictably, the wheels were rolling through the snow-blessed grounds of the forest. The shape of the black pumpkin appeared ominously through the trees and Jarvis was back with his carriage mended and his horse in fine fettle.

'Well, how interesting,' said Jarvis, announcing himself. 'A little party and I'm not invited. What have we here, Mister Roach?'

'Well, in these hands I have the McCreedy boy,' said Roach, pulling the child into view with his two left arms. 'And in these hands I have our friend Captain Dooley.' He grinned with the wooden doll held preciously on display.

It was the first time Jarvis had seen children since the others had escaped him. He stared in disbelief, unable to comprehend how Roach had managed to capture one before he had. He was mesmerized by its ugliness. The little round face, the snubby little nose. The sheer smallness of it. Chalky white skin, that had not been blessed with sunlight. They really were dreadful creatures.

Jarvis was not the only one inspecting Edgar closely. Faces leered down at him. Long snouts and dribbling mouths seemed to draw closer and closer. By now he was coming to his senses, wondering where he was and what strange company he was keeping.

'An impressive catch indeed,' said Jarvis, whose insane jealousy was immediately overridden by his joy that Captain Dooley had been discovered. It was so long since he'd worn the expression that the smile he made almost cracked his face in half.

'Who are you, boy?' he sneered.

'Edgar,' he said in a mumbled daze. 'Edgar McCreedy.'

'Oh really,' he said, staring harder. 'Huh ... I must look harder in future, eh,' he mumbled to himself.

'Take him to the undergate,' said Hogwick and a procession of four- and two-legged things marched Edgar away.

Jarvis took hold of the wooden soldier. It was their first meeting. Jarvis found it hard to believe that this loose-limbed scrap of wood and rusting joints, with his pointy little nose and round rolling eyes, could help him. 'We shall see,' he whispered to himself and he tucked him into his belt so that the Captain's head and arms hung over the leather and across the buckle. He climbed back onto his carriage and left.

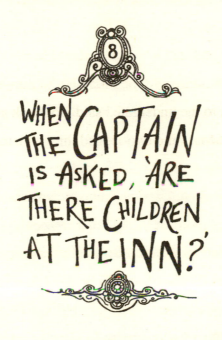

WHEN THE CAPTAIN IS ASKED, 'ARE THERE CHILDREN AT THE INN?'

Captain Dooley's way of speaking was more than strange.

There was to be no hesitation on Jarvis's part. Everyone knew where his first suspicions lay. Excitement thumped in his heart as he popped the old wooden soldier on the mantelpiece. He had prepared himself for the moment by making himself a drink and lighting the fire, almost as if he was about to enjoy a favourite book or sit down to a hearty meal. Esther sat on the top of the wingbacked chair with her feet clamped into the dirty fabric. She could see that her position was about to be made redundant. With Captain Dooley's knowledge of where all the children were, it seemed she would be without use, but knowing she could do nothing, she hung around until she was forced to do otherwise.

Now there are some things that don't seem right no matter how you look at them. You can see the proof right there in front of you. But somehow, it is not enough. And that was exactly how it felt to watch and listen to Captain Dooley speaking. He would drop his square little box of a lower jaw like it was springloaded and the words would come tumbling out in the meanest, croakiest, most pathetic little voice you've ever heard.

Jarvis took a noisy slurp of the drink that he held with his right hand. The hook was curled around the mug handle, not holding it, just leaning on it.

'Are there children at the Deadman's Hand?'

Captain Dooley spat out the words, 'Three little

birds at the Deadman's Hand.' Once he'd said it, that was it. There was no going back. Those children would be hunted day and night.

And it was only then that the likeness became apparent to Jarvis.

'Of course, Esther, of course,' he said, rising to his feet and staring into the air as if lost in thought. 'I have had a moment of clarity!' He smiled.

His mind went back to the portrait. It was the landlord's face but younger. Of course it was. It was his son. And the three little birds were the two boys and the girl, all hiding together at the tavern!

The full realization made him momentarily happy but within a breath, happiness boiled into fury.

There are times when anger overtakes you. Destroys every piece of common sense you have and every piece of logic in your brain. That's what happened to Jarvis when he heard the children were at the Deadman's Hand. Why had he been so careful? Why had he trodden so lightly, with all those months of wondering suspiciously about the place? How dare they go behind his back? How could they lie to him so blatantly?

How dare they ignore his importance!

He should have just done it there and then, he thought, and of course, he hadn't. But he was going to do it now. It was time to instill some fear into these people. Time to show them how ruthless he was and how far he was prepared to go to get what he wanted.

He left the house with the task burning away in his mind. He would do it whatever happened. Esther would have joined him but he slammed the door before she could glide out after him and she was left pecking at the window pane, only to be ignored. With the reigns held in his hooked hand he carried a flaming torch to light the way. Often the bay mare would bear the brunt of his anger – taking a scolding or pushed beyond her limits through his frustration.

They moved off, Jarvis shouting at the horse as they went. The carriage wound into action, the back wheel turning swiftly on the repaired axle, crunching and grinding through the packed snow. It ploughed through the streets, slipping and sliding in and out of the corners, all the way to the Deadman's Hand.

There is an old alley that runs down the back of the

tavern and from there is the back door that leads inside. The barrels there are stacked high and low, so much so that it is difficult to pass at times.

Jarvis made one simple move that was to change everything in an instant. He took the burning torch and he held it to the barrels that lay stacked against the doorway. At first it didn't catch. The wood was frosted and the flames licked and licked but they couldn't take a hold. And then he kicked one until the inside was shattered and exposed. That was all it took. The fire met the empty rum barrel and flames whooshed into the air, smothering the confined space with instant heat and combustion. Orange glowed and billowed and suddenly everything was being swallowed up. The fire spread to the doorframe and now it ate along the structural timbers that held the inn together.

It crackled and spat and roared. The external shutters collapsed in the heat, crashing inwards, destroying the panes and taking flames with them. Jarvis just stood and watched as if in some kind of weird trance. Immediately, the fire spread across the kitchen and began to work its way through the house.

It was a crazy move. Without flinching, Jarvis walked down the alley out into the open street and watched as the tenants of the Deadman's Hand awakened to the disaster. The whole city could have gone up, taking the forest with it. The orange flicker reflected in the evil of Jarvis's eyes, the torch still held in his hand. When the children emerged he would take all three of them, and he would show no mercy.

WHEN THE SAFETY OF THE TAVERN IS REPLACED BY THE DANGER OF THE STREETS

It is true what they say: 'fire is neither friend nor foe'. It was the panes of glass smashing and not the fire itself that woke Frankie. But when she did wake she could hear the crackle and roar billowing through the building. She sneaked a look from the window. Glowing orange flecks danced and drifted and black smoke obscured the view. A peek along the corridor confirmed her suspicions. She couldn't see anything but the noise was much louder and unmistakable.

She woke the boys with furious shakes. 'Out, out! Get out! The inn is on fire!' she cried and the boys, half awake, half still sleeping, were thrown headlong into the action.

Sam was the same, snoring away like a rhino. She bashed at the door and screamed, running to his side and shaking it to wake him. He felt solid and soft at the same time, like a large lump of dough. Soon he was up and quickly away on his feet, taking her with him.

All those escape plans they had in place had taken no account of the fact that they all slept like babies and could barely be woken.

The four of them met on the corridor.

'To the cellar,' instructed Sam, still pulling on his

clothes. He herded the children down the staircase before him, squeezing along behind, finding it difficult to get his huge frame moving quickly down the narrowness of the walkway.

'Faster!' cried Pip, who was pulling at Toad's shirt and listening to his panting as he went.

'I can't see!' yelled Frankie. She was at the front now and feeling her way along the walls in the dark. The heat was forcing its way through the partition and making her hands warm. Pip tugged at her clothing, sensing his way forward, and Toad continued to breathe down his ear. They fumbled at the corners and now they were only seconds away from the kitchen – but it was being swallowed up in the fire and so the way to the cellar was blocked.

That meant only one thing. There was no chance of an escape into the catacombs beneath. Their perfect route into the Hollow was shut off. There would be no taking the boat through the bricked arches beneath the streets. No escape through the drain holes into the city above.

Sam's instinct was to keep the children safe, but

their home was burning. A thick fug of black smoke piped out through the closed kitchen door. The door blistered with the heat. It was about to give way.

Toad urged them down the passage towards the side door that lead down the alleyway to the street. There was no choice. 'Don't go yet, wait for my signal!' Sam shouted after them in panic. 'Once you're out, keep your heads down and stay safe. Get to the catacombs and find shelter. Don't stay down there, it's far too cold. Get to Finn Shaw's or Ben Turnwheel's or somewhere safe.'

Sam peeked out through the door and felt the icy temperature hit him like a wall. The Hollow was colder now than it had ever been. Right through to the skin, cold. With blankets and hoods wrapped around them the children stood back in the darkness of the porch. Sam looked down into the back alley. Black smoke was choking the passageway and obscuring the view momentarily. It was a good time to move.

He escorted the children towards the open road into the city and insisted they keep themselves tucked into the shadows of the tall buildings.

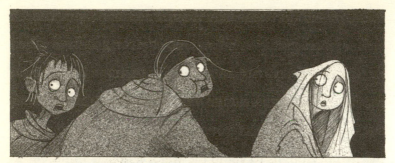

'Be safe,' cried Toad under the crackling sounds of the flames.

'I'll be fine,' said Sam. 'Go! And hurry.'

Moments later he was in the back street. He was joined by city folk. Out in their night clothes. smashing the frozen troughs to get to the water and half filling what was left of the discarded barrels, passing it along the line to Sam, who poured it in through the window. The stacks of barrels were prized and kicked apart and it helped to lessen the impact. Snow was hurled in heaps and handfuls.

Sam stopped to take a breath. He did not know that Jarvis preyed silently at the scene. Lurking in wait for the children emerging and not realizing that the black smoke his fire had created was the very thing that had allowed them to get away.

The distant cries of the firefighters was drifting. To avoid a clutch of witches circling overhead, Toad had brought the children almost full circle and now they were almost back where they started. But he would take them to a point where he knew there was a drain cover.

From here they could escape into the catacombs below.

Not far to go. Except that when they reached the right point, something was parked over the wooden drain cover. Something squat and round and black with huge wheels and a fat body.

'Jarvis!' whispered Pip. 'He's waiting for us to emerge.' He was back in his carriage and poised for action.

'Crafty old snake,' said Toad. 'I think we've found our firestarter.'

'How do we get to the drain?' asked Frankie. But the only way was to find another one nearby.

Captain Dooley was now sitting perched in Jarvis's lap and he was beginning to feel that something was nearby. He felt the words coming from inside him.

'Three little birds, sitting on a log,' he sang, in his pathetic, scratchy little voice. But he was drowned out by the crackling and roaring of the fire and Jarvis's trancelike state.

All the while the fire was raging and the city folk were throwing what they could find of water and snow on to the flames. It could have been a stroke of luck or it could have been pure magic but just at that moment a huge drift of snow broke from the roof and slid down, smothering the flames with soft white. Maybe the heat inside was rising up through the roof and had released it. Maybe the weight of the snowdrift had sent it sliding. Whatever caused it was a mystery, but it was enough to quell the fire outside and the folk went in to tackle the parlour where the stores were burning wildly.

Jarvis moved off, feeling impatient and somehow convincing himself that if he kept circling, perhaps he would come across the children.

Toad knew where every drain cover lay in the whole of the city. But the thick snow only served to confuse him. He couldn't find a single one and they scrambled around in the dark, hiding among the piles of firewood and broken barrels to avoid being seen by Jarvis. Eventually, the one he had been seeking was right there, and he scratched away with cold hands. But the lid was frozen, stuck to the ground and refusing to budge. Pip tried to breathe on the seal of ice, as if to loosen the frozen grip, but it wasn't going anywhere for the time being.

They slipped into shadows, making a quick succession of turns through a maze of houses, and suddenly they were at a low doorway. Who knew what was about to greet them – friend or foe?

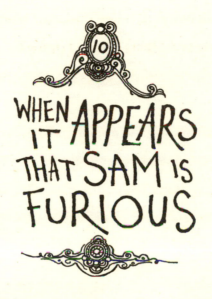

WHEN IT APPEARS THAT SAM IS FURIOUS

Sam stood back in the alleyway. Thick smoke was rising quickly upwards but the fire was out. He had the villagers to thank. That and the stroke of luck delivered in the form of a rooftop avalanche.

It was times like this when Sam realized there was a strong community spirit bubbling under the chill winds of the Hollow. The people who passed his window and stayed buttoned up in their homes under the snow were out there, heart and soul, when he fell into trouble.

He looked around himself. There they all were. Covered in black smoke, coughing and choking. Some of them drenched in the water they had been passing to and fro and now frozen with it. If they ever rid this place of all its woes there was a great city beneath its evil crust.

The damage was bad enough, but Sam would get by. He had been through worse than this. It seemed that the fire had begun in the back alley. That was where it had burned the longest, the barrels reduced to nothing but crumbling charcoal. A fire

in the alley when the streets were filled with winter snow! It could only be deliberate. He was furious. His mind tracked back, wondering if he had upset anyone at the tavern. And then he remembered the scene with Jarvis. The frustrated outburst, the raid on the premises and now the fire. Were those things connected? Maybe!

It was time to have words with Mister Jarvis.

EXPLAINING WHETHER THE NAME 'FLOYD' SPELLS FRIEND OR FOE

Toad pushed down on the latch. It was open. It was not the first time he had chanced upon an open doorway and he knew that to do so here in the Hollow was to take a life-threatening chance. But what could they do?

They stepped in, their three faces appearing around the frame of the door. The room was in darkness and the only light that came was from blackened coals and logs crumbling into a relaxed warmth in a stone-built hearth.

'Quick, get in and shut the door,' said Toad.

They shuffled forward, banging the snow from their boots and calling out gently, but no one came. For a moment they peered through the curtains at the small square panes of the window.

Jarvis rattled past in the black pumpkin. He seemed to slow up at the window and the three of them almost jumped from their skins when his leering face appeared to stare right in. Surely he hadn't spotted them? They shrank back from their positions at the curtain and coiled themselves up into a corner. It wasn't until they could hear the wheels of the carriage rolling forward again that they breathed a united sigh of relief.

They crouched in the hearth, warming their frozen fingers in the orangey glow.

'Where are we?' asked Frankie.

'How do I know?' said Toad. 'Someone's house.'

'Well, we can't just make ourselves at home. It could belong to anybody. We might be in great danger,'

insisted Pip.

'Just being here in the first place means we're in great danger, doesn't it? It's nothing new,' grinned Toad.

Just then the latch lifted at the door and the children froze. A long lean bespectacled man entered, bringing a heavy smell of wood smoke with him. He shook his coat tail, removing a long scarf that was bundled about his neck, and then he sat in his chair to kick off his snow-filled boots. When he looked up he saw the children, silent and staring back at him.

'Holy witchwood!' he

said, holding on to his heart and almost leaping backwards through the seat of his chair. 'Where did you spring from?' And then, squinting through his glasses in the dark, he took a closer look at Toad as his hands gripped his armchair in startled fright. 'Well, bless my soul, you're Sam's boy, aren't ya?'

'Yes, sir, and we're sorry to intrude but Mister Jarvis was after us, sir. We didn't mean no harm.'

The man jumped to his feet and took a nervous check on the street outside. 'Now look here, children,' he began, 'I don't mind helping out, really I don't, but I could be in serious trouble for harbouring youngsters. You realize that, don't you?' He scraped his hair back and rubbed his chin. He was tall and light on his feet and somehow all his limbs seemed too long and loose, as if he had been badly put together. He was the nervous type, the kind that can't seem to stop shuffling when they're talking.

'I can't put you up,' he said, 'no way.' And then as soon as he had said it he changed his mind. 'OK, I'll do it,' he returned, 'but not for long. I've been helping your father put out the fire,' he said, turning to Toad again.

'It wasn't easy. There are good people here among these darkened streets. They all helped. It's out now, your father is safe. He's a good man, your father, and I'll help him as much as I can, I will, and if that means keeping you here, I'll do it. That's what we do here. We help each other.' It was almost as if he was telling himself to do it as he spoke. As if he needed to convince himself of his actions.

The children breathed a sigh of relief. They had had no control over the extinguishing of the fire and had watched helplessly from the labyrinth of alleyways.

'My name's Floyd,' said the man, 'Percival Floyd. But you can call me Percy.' And as he asked the children their names he put water in a pan over the burning embers and stoked up the fire with fresh wood. 'I'll make us a warm drink, eh, that should sort you out.' Toad instinctively pulled on the shutters and Pip and Frankie hung their wet clothes by the hearth. 'I never had children of my own,' he continued, 'I was never married. I'm a simple man. But I'm a good cook,' he insisted and he brought another pot into the room. This one was filled with a wonderful-smelling stew and as it warmed at the stove the room filled with the aroma. 'I know it's a strange hour to eat,' he said, but it will do you good to get something warm down you. All that time out in the snow will have frozen the bones.' He laughed.

They sat and talked through the early hours and it seemed Mister Floyd was full of knowledge about Hangman's Hollow. Even more so than Toad, Pip thought. And perhaps, after all his concerns, he was actually enjoying the company that he craved in the times he was alone. At length, daylight poured through the gaps in the shutters and the children disappeared to a secret spot to get some rest as Floyd sat back in his chair and closed his eyes. Just for now, they would all stay still.

There was no reason at all why Jarvis would suspect they hid at Percival Floyd's house, was there?

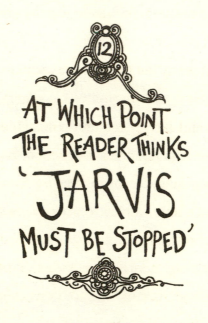

AT WHICH POINT THE READER THINKS 'JARVIS MUST BE STOPPED'

There was a soft grey blue light at the end of the day that signalled more snow. It had stayed freezing cold and icicles stared down from above, pointing at the passers-by.

But it took more than mere cold weather to keep Mister Jarvis from the streets. And now that he had Captain Dooley in his possession he was all too keen to venture out.

To Mister Jarvis, it was the perfect evening. Captain Dooley was tucked into his belted waist and the two of them were setting out into the heart of Hangman's Hollow. As the wheels of the black pumpkin began to turn, small flakes of white began to fall around them. It was postcard pretty but things were about to grow a little hectic.

Where would Jarvis head first? He had lost sight of those rats from the Deadman's Hand, but for now there must be plenty more for the picking.

'Tell me, Captain Dooley. Where might the nearest of our dear children be? It would be so good to furnish our cabin with city rats. It has been so long since I plucked one from its nest. Speak to Mister Jarvis, Captain, and make him happy.'

'Where the river swallows up the broken bridge. One little bird in the rounded roof,' croaked the Captain.

A smile broke across Jarvis's face. This was going to be so easy. Plucked like fruit from ripened trees.

He considered it hard, his eyes staring upwards in thought. He kept moving the carriage forward and then as he realized he knew where the Captain was sending him he slowly pulled on one side of the reins, yanking a steady left-hand turn and sliding gently until he faced the other way.

A little further and he'd be in a good position to get a view of where he headed.

He steered up and around the corner to take in the view of where he knew the timbers of an old walkway had sunk into the stinking river. From the stone bridge he could see it: a wooden construction that had long since collapsed halfway across the water, as if unable to make the distance. Its rotted wooden struts stuck out like broken fingers and at the bank side was a small circular building: home to Mrs Duvell. Though Jarvis had presumed she lived alone she was obviously harbouring an escapee.

He set off again and savoured the moment, the carriage swaying and rocking across the snow-topped cobbles as he wound back down to the other side of the river. As he neared he could see a wisp of smoke pipe up from the chimney pot, and though the shutters were tight across the window, a slice of light peeped out from within.

'How dare she!' he whispered to himself. 'How dare she lie to me and keep those rats from my sight.' He pulled up just short of the rounded house.

He climbed down from the carriage seat, wandered to the back and, confident of his catch, opened the lock and positioned the prison door ajar, ready for its first victim.

He announced himself with three slow loud knocks at the door. *Thud, thud, thud.*

'Little pig, little pig, let me come in,' he sang to himself.

A frail and frightened-looking woman came quickly. But it was not the time of night to receive visitors, especially in such harsh weather. She partially opened the door, just enough to poke her face out into the light of Jarvis's torch.

'Yes?' she answered.

'Mrs Duvell?' enquired Jarvis, wearing his kindest grin.

'Yes.'

'And how are we this evening?'

'I'm fine, thank you, Mister Jarvis.' She stared at

him, confused by his mild-mannered approach combined with the lateness of the hour.

'Can I help you with something?' she asked.

'Oh, I wouldn't have thought so, Mrs Duvell. It's the children I'm seeking. The young ones. City rats, I call them. Everywhere, they are. One just needs to know where to look, I think.'

'Yes, quite. Well, if I see anything I'll be sure to tell you,' she urged and she attempted to prise the opening shut. But Jarvis's foot was wedged in the jamb of the door.

'You sure you don't have anything for me, Mrs Duvell?'

'Quite sure,' she smiled, nodding her head, and again she tried to force his foot out from the door frame.

Jarvis came close to her frightened face and stared hard.

'I'm feeling generous, seeing as the weather has delivered a pleasant evening.'

He looked round over his shoulder, as if he was about to share a secret with the lady at the doorway. And then, in hushed tones he continued.

'Mrs Duvell, if you don't bring that child out here in the next five minutes I'll be delivering you to the authorities. If you do as I ask, I shall forget where I found the little urchin and I'll expect you to thank me for it. Do I make myself clear?'

She stared at him for a good while longer, saying nothing. Then the door closed and the latch could be heard returning to its place. Jarvis stood and waited. There were noises. Muffled voices and movement. Up and down steps. Doors banging. A dog barked in the distance on the other side of town and then others came, as if calling to each other. Jarvis had not realized how long five minutes was. He was not known for his patience. He was about to bang at the door again when it opened fully. A small frightened boy appeared with a handful of belongings and a drip-white face. He was long-haired and scruffy and Jarvis took a step backwards at the sight of him. Mrs Duvell retreated into the parlour, staring out at Jarvis with tears streaming down her face.

'Please don't hurt him, Mister Jarvis. He's not mine. He's the son of Mister Brice. He's a good boy. Never did nobody no harm.'

75

'Why, thank you, Mrs Duvell, how very obliging of you. I'm sure he'll be just fine. Now that was easy, wasn't it? May I remind you that children are banned in the Hollow. Good day.' And he shut the door in her face.

Jarvis curled his hook into the shoulder of the boys' tunic and yanked him out into the street, dragging him to the carriage. He forced him inwards and locked the door soundly and the last thing Mrs Duvell heard was Jarvis shouting at the horse to get back up the small climb to the city road.

The smile had stayed across Jarvis's face. He was so delighted with his catch that he stopped to take another look. Pausing at the stone bridge, he climbed down and walked to the back of the carriage. He peered in through the window and he could just see the shape of the small boy, his watery eyes glistening under the torchlight.

'How sickly sweet,' he laughed and then he climbed back into his seat.

'Where next?' he asked his friend Captain Dooley.

And then the spooky croaking voice came again, loud and clear.

'Born of the same hour and only a moment away. The Carraway twins are asleep in their beds.'

'My, oh my. Mister and Mrs Carraway. How surprising. All that time she lay in bed with the fever. Such a deceiving plot. She bore no illness at all, it seems. Surprising what people will do to conceal children in the womb,' Jarvis said, chattering away to himself. And then he steered his carriage towards the riverside houses.

But then he was corrected.

'Not at the Carraway house. They fear the searches and sometimes at night, the children are in the care of the DeGale family, along the track where the watermill sits. Below the bridge.'

'Ahhh, I see. They're so sly, but so am I,' laughed Jarvis and he was having so much fun he had forgotten how freezing cold the air had become.

Within moments he was parked up again and rapping at the door with his hook. *Thud, thud, thud.*

But not every taking was going to be so simple. Mister Jarvis was about to meet with much younger and bigger opposition. Mister DeGale was not so much a pushover as the last one. His large frame almost filled out the space as he opened the door.

Jarvis was not perturbed. He informed Mister DeGale that he was about to get into hot water if he didn't hand over the Carraway children.

'Who told you, Jarvis? You'd have to get past me to get to those children, anyway,' insisted DeGale.

Jarvis took one long look up at the man before him, square-jawed and broad in the shoulder. Hmmm, he would have to think for a moment. What would melt this man's ice-cold bravery?

'It's a battle of wits is it, Mister DeGale? Very well. Let me show you something.' He fiddled with the lock of his back door and pulled out the young boy.

'Have you met Mister Brice's youngest son?' he asked. 'I'm presuming Mister Brice would like to see him again, but if you don't bring out those twins I'll have you explain to him what happened to his beloved child.' As he said this he held the boy with his hooked hand over the side of the bridge, ready to let him drop. The boy screamed out loud and then his cry fell to a quiet, pleading blubber of help.

'He's quite heavy. I can't imagine I'll hold on much longer. I don't play games, Mister DeGale. You'd best hurry up.'

DeGale dropped his head in defeat. He had the might to crush Jarvis but he did not have his evil will. He returned quickly with the Carraway twins. 'Don't hurt them, Jarvis. They've done nothing wrong. Keep them safe or I'll come looking for you.'

'Thank you, Mister DeGale,' Jarvis shouted as he left in high spirits. 'Room for a few more, Captain Dooley.' He grinned. This was the best night he had had in a long while.

The next brought problems: a young girl with too much fight in her. A kicker and a screamer. Guards approached through the darkness. 'Do you need help, Mister Jarvis?'

She was biting and pulling at Jarvis's hair and tearing his cloak. 'Let me go! Let me go!'

The guards jumped from their horses but the snow was making it hard underfoot and somehow the girl slipped through their hands, her parents shouting after her, 'Run Shira, run!'

'You'll hang for this!' called Jarvis to her parents. 'After her!' he instructed the guards. But she was lost in the maze of alleyways.

Forced into a bad frame of mind, Jarvis decided he would take the children he had and return later. 'Plenty of time,' he told himself. Three in one night was a good catch considering he hadn't caught one in such a long time. He was determined to outdo Roach and return with much more than he had managed.

And that would have been the end of his night's searching but for a small diversion.

'Where oh where are those children from the tavern?' he said to himself, scratching away at his chin and sneering all around him.

'Three little birds at Mister Floyd's!' croaked the old wooden soldier.

'Oh, really!' said Jarvis as a surprised smile cut across his face. 'Why didn't you tell me, my wooden friend?'

'Captain Dooley should be seen and not heard. Only speak when spoken to. There's a good boy.'

Jarvis looked down at him. He really was an odd

little fellow, even for someone from a place as strange as Hangman's Hollow. He diverted the steer of the carriage in the opposite direction.

'Then we shall call there on the way home. It would be nice to catch up with our friend Percival Floyd after so long,' he said as his evil grin gave way to his crooked teeth.

It was the very sound of those carriage wheels that woke Pip, Toad and Frankie. All three of them had come to know that noise only too well. Its distinct, rumbling, rattling, loose-in-its-frame trundle had made them sit upright in their resting places. Pip had to rub his eyes. What on earth had brought Jarvis to the door?

'Is it him?' said Frankie.

'You don't even have to tell me,' said Toad. 'I know that sound too well.'

'Floyd must be in league with him,' said Pip. 'He must have said something. Somehow sent him a message.' He was rubbing at the window to clear the frost and take a clearer view.

'No, definitely not,' said Toad. 'Floyd is a true friend to my father. He has been for a lifetime. Something else brings him here.'

'Look,' said Pip, 'in the back of the carriage. There are children.' And they craned their necks to get a view of what stood beneath the cottage window.

'You're right. But I can see something far worse than that,' said Toad. 'I hope I'm wrong.'

'What is it?' gasped the others.

'It's Captain Dooley,' announced Toad. 'Jarvis is wearing him at his waist.'

And for the first time, they saw a brief glimpse of Captain Dooley and discovered that he was in the possession of Jarvis. Nothing could be more dangerous. Nothing could put them at more risk and harm than this. How on earth had he discovered the old wooden soldier?

A huge crash came from below as Jarvis made his entry. The door buckled open, taking Floyd by complete surprise as he lay snoozing in his chair.

'Bring them to me,' snarled Jarvis. 'Bring them all.' He was still gasping from the effort of his dramatic entry.

But, I ... I ...' stuttered Floyd, unable to find the words.

From upstairs, only muffled shouts were heard. The children panicked, picking up their things.

'There's no one here. Only me,' insisted Floyd, but then Jarvis's eyes fell upon the four empty bowls in the hearth and without saying anything more he stormed upstairs, flinging back the doors to the rooms and stabbing his hook into the bedcovers in case the children hid beneath. He turned out the cupboards and drawers, swearing that when the Captain told him something, it was true, and that was all the proof he needed.

And then he flung open another door and saw a scene to make his blood boil: an open window and beyond it, small footsteps disappearing into the alleyways. They were gone. They had escaped him yet again.

Jarvis let out a
scream and returned to
the front door.
'Remember my
promise, Percival
Floyd,' he said. 'You
will swing at the
gallows for this.'
And then he was off
into the night.

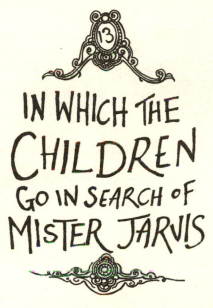

IN WHICH THE CHILDREN GO IN SEARCH OF MISTER JARVIS

Some things make you run until you are so tired you have to stop. But some make you feel so frightened that you run and run and run and you keep on running until it hurts. Your heart is pounding so hard that it feels like it might burst right out of your chest. And all the time you are tripping and falling, slipping and sliding, like in some strange dream. You are completely out of breath, but still you carry on.

In their desperate panic to escape Captain Dooley, the children did just that. They scattered through the streets like wild dogs, scrambling through the pinched footpaths between the houses, so frantic were they to escape the searching mind of Captain Dooley and the sharpened grip of the hook-handed man. If they kept moving they would keep the Captain thinking and make it harder for him, they were sure. They pulled at the drain covers as they went but not a single one would release its grip of ice. They had little time to spend forcing one open and so their escape found them perched beneath a crumbling bridge that spanned a narrow stretch of the river. Their hot breath billowed upwards like smoke from a chimney. The water was frozen solid but to cross it was to expose themselves to open space. They sat a while and huddled together in the cold until they were brave enough to move again.

Pip stared out across the ice. His eyes opened a little wider. 'I have an idea,' he said and he began to explain his thoughts to Toad and Frankie.

There is a part of the Hollow known as the Devil's

Tongue. It's an old dilapidated bridge that crumbles away before the foot timbers collapse into the now frozen water. Beyond the river, on the other side, is a tall structure that is home to the authorities. And in the basement below is the home of our very own Mister Jarvis. A small hovel. Mean and meagre to suit the host.

If you had been stood right there at the Devil's Tongue as the light was dropping away that night, you might just have seen three children sneaking their way under the broken bridge timbers to get a good look. Quite something to see children in the Hollow, braving the open air and taking their chances. Who knew who might see them and spread the word?

So it was with great care that they moved silently along their way. They needed to be sure that the low basement was the home of the man they knew as Jarvis. They were perched in the wooden frame now, sitting upon their perches like preying birds.

It seemed somehow absurd that though they had spent the night escaping from Jarvis and his wooden assistant, they were now, through the early hours, doing exactly the opposite and getting as close to him as possible.

They had seen the black pumpkin parked up outside. With its lantern still burning at the corner, a smudge of dank yellow light kept the doorway illuminated, reflecting its glow upon the icy river. Everything was still. An owl hooted softly in the distance and the gentle creak of trees in the breeze was the only other noise to be heard.

The three of them shook off their anxieties, looked at one another and nodded again.

It was now or never. With heavy hearts they crossed the river on the thick ice that rested like a pie crust on the water. It was cold, so very, very cold. Every now and then the surface heaved a great sigh and cracked beneath their feet. But they knew it would not break through. It was far too thick.

Pip's plan to break into Jarvis's home and take Captain Dooley was more than ambitious to say the least, but they were desperate. Jarvis would be sleeping – after all, he had had the busiest day in a long while. With the Captain at large the children could not run and hide. He was always around the corner, keeping them running, endlessly chasing until he had them in his grasp. If they captured him they could turn the whole situation around and find the lost children of the Hollow, and they could move in secrecy again.

They approached gingerly.

The door was locked but it sat so loose in its frame that they were able to push the bottom half inwards and squeeze through the gap. It felt almost as cold inside as out but a small fire lay dying in the hearth and lit the room softly.

A wingbacked chair sat close to the fireplace, but the room was sparsely furnished and there was little else to speak of apart from piles of papers and books, candlesticks and grog bottles.

They searched the room carefully in the half-light, their hearts drumming together nervously as they quickly became familiar with their surroundings. What looked like a small room adjoined but it was nothing more than a narrow passageway leading to a staircase. It no doubt led to Jarvis, who would be snoring in his bed. Did he have Captain Dooley at his side?

Pip stopped short in the hearth. He was sure that from the mantelpiece two eyes shone back at him through the darkness, staring intently.

There was no mistaking those mystical moons. Even to those who had never seen them, they announced their importance immediately. Yellow white, unblinking in the orange glow from the fire. It was Captain Dooley. Perched right there on the mantel. Offered to them like a gift.

But as they stood entranced by the sight of Captain Dooley someone had been woken from his dreams of escaping city rats. He rose from his bed and tiptoed across the floor. And only moments later, a hooked hand lifted the latch on the crooked staircase door.

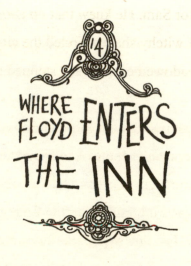

WHERE FLOYD ENTERS THE INN

Floyd had pulled on a long coat and stepped into his boots at the doorway. A woolly skullcap was tugged tightly over his greying hair, covering his ears and the nape of his neck. He stepped out into the night, tucking his gloveless hands into his pockets as he felt the first crunch of snow beneath his feet. A chill wind sent swirls of white circling around him. With his head down he made the familiar walk to the Deadman's Hand. The streets were noisier than usual. The forest was alive with excitement. Children were on the move, desperate to escape the wisdom of the little wooden soldier. It was not a good night to be out, but Floyd had information for Sam. He knew that up above, silhouettes of witchy shapes circled the city streets. He kept to the shadowed corners and stepped out into the night.

When he entered the inn Floyd found that it was busy. But it was without the revelry that the place was accustomed to. There was no music or singing, no raised cheers and forced laughter to forget the dark secrets of the Hollow. Instead, all that were there were stood together, as if in council, huddled at the bar and speaking in hushed tones. They had fallen silent on hearing the door go, but on seeing that it was Floyd they stirred again and he was handed a tankard of ale. The discussion was without doubt about the concerns of the Hollow.

'I need to explain something to you,' said Floyd, his hand resting on Sam's shoulder as he checked around him to make sure their conversation was in secret.

'Don't worry,' said Sam. 'We're all friends here. No secrecy needed.'

'Very well. Your boy was safe with me but they left. All three of them. I could not stop them. I had a visit from Jarvis. He must have had a tip-off. He is less than happy.'

'Really? You've seen my boy. And the others. They're OK?'

The group listened in and showed their concern.

'Well, I hope so,' replied Floyd. 'They had no choice but to disappear into the night. I'm sorry I don't have more to tell you.'

'It's a relief, at least, to know

they are still out there and not in the clutches of the forest,' said Sam. 'It was Jarvis that started the fire, I'm sure. And he wouldn't have done it for no reason. He knew something, somehow. Do you know where they went?'

'No idea. They moved quickly. We had no chance to talk.'

'They know not to return here,' said Sam. 'Maybe they do right to keep on the move. It's not safe to stay still. Not now.'

Shortly after, the McCreedys entered. Mrs McCreedy had not handled it well since her son went missing in the night. She was visibly shaken and looked sick. Her husband held on to her tightly.

'Any news of our boy?' he asked.

'Nothing,' said Sam. 'I'm sorry.'

'This is your doing,' said Mrs McCreedy. 'Hiding children in this place. Attracting unwanted attention. Stirring the forest folks. We 'eard you took a boy in. A stray.'

'Of course,' said Sam. 'I make no apologies. What if I had seen your boy in the street and taken him in.

Would you still have thought it was the wrong thing to do?'

Mrs McCreedy looked at Sam with tears in her eyes. Unable to answer his question, she turned and left, with Mr McCreedy following on after.

'Sam, I'm sorry. I know it's not your fault. Elsa, please,' he shouted after her.

'It's fine, Ely,' said Sam, 'I understand. My own boy is missing too now and I can only hope he is safe. I understand the frustration. I share your anger. This place is becoming a living nightmare. Keep talking to me. We must all of us keep talking.'

Much more was said that night. Fighting talk. The kind to send a shiver down the spine and raise the hackles. The type of speak that raises hair on the back of the neck and brings goosebumps to the surface of the skin. Of taking up arms and challenging the forest. Of pitchforks and spears and handmade weapons. Plans that spoke of fire and flames, blades and bayonets.

There were tears too and high emotions. Lost children are the worst fear of parents. To conceal your greatest treasure is one thing. To have it taken is another.

Sam knew the children were no longer safe at the inn. And he knew that he himself was also in danger now. Perhaps the authorities would question him. Sure, they had found nothing in the tavern. But he knew and they knew that a cloud hovered over the Deadman's Hand.

'To all your children,' said Floyd and he raised his tankard aloft. 'That they may one day live in peace.'

'To all our children,' came the reply and all the glasses and tankards were raised in the silence of the Deadman's Hand. A chink of glass and pewter resounded softly amid the crackling of the fire and outside the wind hurled the snow around the eerie streets of the empty Hollow.

AT WHICH POINT SOMEONE IS TAKEN BY SURPRISE

The door opened slowly. Snake eyes pierced the darkness of the room. He lit a candle in the fire and returned the holder to its place on the long wooden table. His nose lifted and he drew in a cloud of air. Strange, he could still smell those damn children. That whiff of youth had always stuck in his nose. But then he noticed something that wasn't right. He returned to the candlestick, picked it up and held it over the mantel. Where was Captain Dooley? His heart thumped back at him in response when he realized the old wooden soldier was missing. He looked down into the hearth. Perhaps he had fallen from his perch. 'No, damn it, where is he?' he swore. He searched around his feet and then angrily threw the candlestick into the fire.

The three children were huddled into the corner. If they held tight he would believe they'd fled and he'd go out into the night to search for them. Wouldn't he?

But they had not noticed that their concealment had been witnessed. Esther stepped out from the darkness of a shelf on the wall where books and papers were stacked.

'They're here,' she said.

'It's the boy from the inn, isn't it. Him and his little cronies. I know it is. I can smell them.'

'The very same,' she answered. 'Delivered to your door, sire.'

'Ahh, bless you, Esther. You still have your uses, eh!' Jarvis grinned and patted her head gently.

She had been there all along. Watching and waiting.

In the low light she had gone unnoticed. Why had they been so careless? Pip was angry with himself. Surely by now he had learnt to wander around the Hollow with his eyes wide open.

Pip and Frankie were curled up with Toad almost sat right on top of them. Pip had Captain Dooley cupped in both hands, holding on to him tight.

Jarvis threw off his cloak and began to search, cursing them as he went. 'Come here, little piggies. Didn't Mummy tell you, it isn't nice to pinch other people's toys.' It was dark but there was little space and not much to search amongst. He would have them by their throats within minutes.

'Come along, my pesky little city rats,' he pleaded. 'Come to Uncle Jarvis.' He was full of excitement. Those kids had haunted his dreams for the past three months. He could not have hoped that they would walk right into his hands. It really was turning out to be the perfect evening.

'Tell me, oh dear Captain, where are the three little birds?'

Pip was too late. He heard the voice coming but he

was so shocked that he was unable to do anything.

'Three little birds, nesting in the cupboard.'

Jarvis moved to the corner of the room. He placed his hook on the large doorknob and flicked it open. A nasty smile announced his delight. Their pathetic, sorrowful little eyes stared up at him. Their wizened little figures curled up in a nest like newborn rats. Shrinking further back into the corner, they shook in fright as Jarvis speared his hook into the wooden panel that formed the back of the cupboard, missing their heads by a fraction.

A bang came at the door. It was so loud that it stopped Jarvis in his tracks. He pushed the cupboard door so that it was almost shut and then he went to uncover the source of the nuisance. Horses could be heard outside and the banging quickly became louder and persistent. Voices followed. Loud shouts. Before Jarvis had reached it, the door came inwards, flying off its hinges and spinning into the space that made the parlour before ending up flat on the floor.

It was none other than Hector Stubbs.

'Jarvis. I have a warrant for your arrest.'

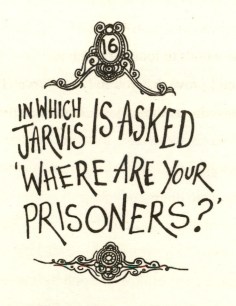

IN WHICH JARVIS IS ASKED 'WHERE ARE YOUR PRISONERS?'

It was a shame that the children were huddled together with their eyes shut. It would have been a treat for them to have seen Jarvis so frightened. He was pinned into a corner with Stubbs staring into his eyes, pressing him firmly and not caring too much for weak excuses.

In the mayhem their presence had gone unnoticed and Toad had slowly pulled the cupboard door shut to conceal their company. Captain Dooley's mouth was held tight.

'Mister Jarvis, do you realize that dealing with the woodsfolk is an act of treason?'

'I haven't dealt with the woodsfolk, sir, I promise. I go to the woods to look for children.'

'When I prove that you're lying, Jarvis, I'll make sure you swing at the gallows. Do you understand me?'

'Yes, sir.'

'I'm going to ask you again, have you delivered children to the forest and taken monies from the woodsfolk?'

'No, sir.'

'Mister Jarvis. You're lying. I can see right through you. You're hollow on the inside, do you know that? Empty-headed. You don't think straight and I'm going to prove it.'

Jarvis tried to remain calm but he was shifting awkwardly on his seat and he was finding it impossible to keep his hands still. He fidgeted with the hem of his cloak.

'Earlier you discovered a young girl in the street. When the parents resisted, holding on to their young one, you were helped by guards, who fended away the adults.'

'Er … yes.'

'And the girl?'

'She escaped through the streets, no thanks to your guardsmen.'

'So you came away empty-handed?'

'Of course.'

'A fruitless night, you might say!'

'If you wish.'

'Don't try make a fool out of me, Jarvis. Where are those children that you already held in your carriage? You certainly didn't bring them to me. I suspect you thought they'd gone unnoticed.'

'I was attacked,' Jarvis claimed. 'By the forest folk.

They took the children from me in the early hours. I was on my way to you.'

'Strange! You never mentioned it!'

'I didn't think I needed to. It happens a lot. I capture children and I get hijacked. It's a dangerous occupation.'

'Oh, really? The last we spoke you said you hadn't seen anything for months!'

Jarvis looked down, thinking hard. Damn it, he was being outsmarted. He was far more used to being the one asking the questions. It wasn't easy the other way round.

'Now tell me, which is the correct story, Mister Jarvis? Because I have a version of my own and I think it's better than yours. I think you have more to do with those forest freaks than you'll admit. And I think that somewhere along the line you get more from delivering to the forest keep than you do to the city! Tell me I'm wrong!'

'Of course you're wrong.'

'Let me remind you of something, Jarvis. You're here to protect the children of this city. I know people don't see you that way but you're there to keep them from harm. I want this city to have a future. Without its children I won't have an army to fight the forest, the city will die out altogether and those tree dwellers will take over when you and I grow old.'

Jarvis didn't have an answer. He didn't see it that way, and if the truth be known he wanted rid of all those children.

Unable to defend his position he was cuffed in irons and taken outside, where transport waited to take him back to the city prison. In panic, Esther followed on behind.

WHEN WE SWITCH TO THE ACTIVITY IN THE FOREST KEEP

17

Silas was perched at the undergate. He kept a watchful eye over the forest keep entrance.

The prisoners were beginning to attract far too much attention. And they were becoming numerous.

Edgar McCreedy

had been joined by the Carraway twins and Mr Brice's son. When word had begun to spread that Captain Dooley was assisting Jarvis, a handful had fled into the streets to escape detection, and been caught as they moved through the city.

Perhaps there were seven or eight now. Maybe more.

It was some time since the forest keep had been home to children. It was a most unpleasant place. The bowels of the forest, deep beneath the trees: a huge underground cavern dug out by the creatures born of the woods. The walls still bore their sinister claw marks and were reminders of just what the children would have to deal with if they attempted escape. Large roots spiralled around the space like wall decorations and fibrous threads of plant life came down from above.

An argument was boiling between the elders of the forest and was overheard by the frightened children. 'Leave them,' said Hogwick. 'They're too valuable alive.' But it was taking a lot to convince some of the bark demons of the forest. Long winters meant that food was not easily available and they were beginning to look at the prisoners with a different eye.

'Perhaps they will be of better use if the winter continues to leave us unfed,' came the wheezing voice of some ungodly creature who stared longingly at the little ones.

'Quiet,' said Hogwick. 'I won't hear of it. Do not give ideas to the others. Their bellies grow hungry and their minds grow weak. They will be easily influenced.'

It was true, there was unrest in the forest. Trouble in the trees was not good for the cause of the woodsfolk. The strength of their union would be their success. Disagreement would not help.

There was much talk between the forest creatures. 'Hunger breeds

anger in the demons,' confided Hogwick. She was in discussion with Roach and Stixx. 'We wield great power over the city with the children alive. But without them we are nothing – back to where we started. Keep your companions alert at all times. Some of our brethren are nothing but animals and think only of food and water. We must keep a careful eye over the keep. The anger of the bark demons needs to be used to our advantage. If they grow more discontent it may be the right time to make an attack and send them into the city.'

'You may be right. We must discuss it with the others,' said Roach.

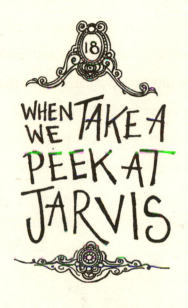

18

WHEN WE TAKE A PEEK AT JARVIS

Esther had neglected to inform the forest of Jarvis's misadventure. Her time was consumed by following the guardsmen and making sure she knew where Jarvis was located. She also wanted to be the only one responsible for his escape. It was important that she won favour with her master. Captain Dooley had been stealing the limelight, telling his tales and allowing Jarvis to pick

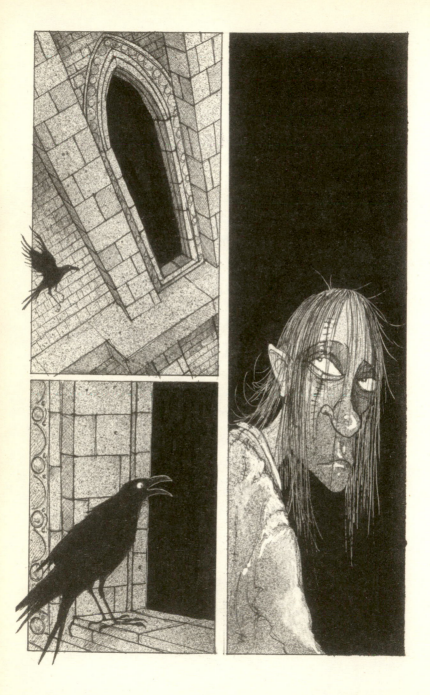

off the children. She must prove her worth and win her place again as his companion.

She found the small window at the top of the hangman's tower, bedded her feet into the snow-trimmed ledge and pushed her face up to the glass. Her large beak pointed downwards, and she used it to scratch away at the frost. She could see something in there. Captain Dooley was no use when it came to escapes. Only she could help.

She felt sure that she could break in. Those little panes of glass would only take so much pecking before they cracked.

Jarvis sat with his head buried in his hands. Just when he had started to make some progress, his whole world had fallen apart again. Things had been perfect. With Captain Dooley sat by his side he had been able to pick off those children from the city and fill the forest keep. Why had he been so careless? It was his own fault, he knew.

If Captain Dooley ended up in the wrong hands those children might survive. Every last one of them. And he hated children so much that just that thought alone brought a tear to his eye.

A cracking sound came from above. He gazed
towards the tall ceiling of the room where he was kept.
A tiny window he hadn't noticed was splintering glass
down on him.

'What … Esther! What are
you doing here?'

Her beak poked
through the
fractured glass
pane and she
turned her head sideways to gaze down upon him.
When she was sure it was him she disappeared again.
She would return with rope and he would be out
within no time at all.

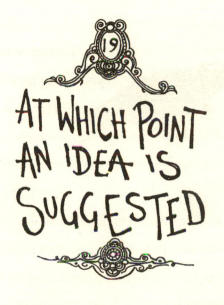

AT WHICH POINT AN IDEA IS SUGGESTED

The children had emerged from their hiding space inside the cupboard and were now taking a good look at Captain Dooley, although they were anxious about making use of him. That horrible little wooden face was not to be trusted, they were sure. But the truth was, Captain Dooley held no discrimination. He just blurted out the truth to whoever asked him.

No one had wanted to touch him. Or look at him. Frankie was brave enough to step up and take hold. She half expected a bite or a nip but to start with, there was nothing from the lifeless character. At first sight, he appeared to be just what he was, a limp and lifeless puppet. But he felt Frankie's grip around him and everything came to him in a breath. 'Little Frances Duprie. Escaping the horrors of the Hollow while her siblings wait in vain.'

Immediately she threw the doll to the floor in shock, her heart quickening.

'I don't want to touch him,' she said.

Pip was emptying a tattered and torn drawstring bag of odds and ends. 'Use this,' he said. Frankie picked the Captain up by his hat and dropped him inside.

For the moment they sat tight in Jarvis's hovel and discussed their plans. With all the fuss of Jarvis being captured they were sure his home would be a safe haven for now.

Toad was wandering around the room and Pip watched him bend down and take something from the floor. He held it up and shook the dust from it. It was

Jarvis's black cloak. He pulled it on and pretended to walk like Jarvis, holding his torch up to the windows and doors, and it got them all laughing, for a moment at least. But Pip could see Toad's mind turning over. He was having serious thoughts – something to do with the cloak itself.

'No!' said Pip.

'It could work,' said Toad.

'What are you talking about?' asked Frankie.

'Follow me,' said Toad and, taking a careful look through the window first, he stepped outside the door, pulled on the cloak and jumped into the carriage seat, taking hold of the reigns in both hands.

'Come along, my pesky little city rats. Come to Mister Jarvis,' said Toad, laughing out loud in his best Jarvis voice.

'Are you serious?' said Pip.

'How else we gonna get into that forest keep?'

'You look too short. Hang on,' said Pip and he jumped aboard, perching on the back of the seat with his legs around Toad's shoulders. He pulled the cloak up higher and yanked the hood over his own head.

Pip looked at Frankie. It was the most terrifying thought that any of them had ever had. But it might be the only thing that could work. It would make for an easy route into the forest and on to the keep.

'It looks OK,' said Frankie with her arms folded, 'but now the legs seem too short! Wait there.' And then she took her turn and squeezed herself on to the end of Toad's legs in the footwell as if to extend the leg area.

'Good thinking,' said Toad and he pulled the cloak across her.

'Are we brave enough to see this through?' said Frankie.

'Are we dumb enough to let those forest gumps walk all over us? Is there a better plan?' asked Toad.

'Come on then. Giddyup, lass,' Pip whispered to the mare and they set off with the carriage rumbling into life, Pip finding his feet with the reins and steering up out of the dip that was home to Jarvis's hovel. He pulled the hood of the cloak well over his face, ensuring he wasn't seen.

'Do you know where we're going?' said Pip.

'Of course I know where I'm going,' said Toad. I've lived here for twelve years. I know these streets better than old Jarvis. Just listen for my directions.'

As the carriage rolled into the city streets, Toad discreetly whispered his route to the forest. They would pass under the central bridge and around the fountain, and then through the pointed arch past the Deadman's Hand and towards the nearby trees. Toad knew he would see the burnt-out remains at the back of the inn, and he knew they would all be tempted to go straight there. To do so was to put them all in great danger and blow their cover. It would take all his willpower not to head through the door and throw his arms around his father.

IN WHICH SAM IS TAKEN BY SURPRISE

In the tall wingbacked chair that was huddled to the burning embers, sat the large figure of Sam. He broke the silence with loud snores.

Sam felt something shake him, and he awoke immediately. At first he stared unknowingly. He said nothing but he held his arm out and touched Toad's face. He looked up to see that Frankie and Pip were by his side. He stared for a while and the four of them stayed silent, all looking at each other. 'Is it really you, son? I thought I'd lost you!'

Sam sat up in his chair. He was still half asleep and confused.

'Welcome back,' said Sam. 'I thought I'd lost you for good. It's not been the same without you. I miss having you around. Are you well? Did you come to any harm? It's not safe here, you do know that, don't you? You can't stay, son.'

The children stared back at him. They said nothing. And then, just like before, they faded away into emptiness. They had never been there at all. It was another fevered dream. They seemed to grow more and more regular. For sure it was

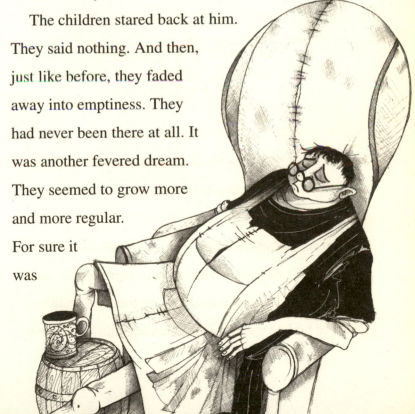

Sam's anxieties that led him to his nightmares, but each night he would awake and think that they were right there before him. Then the realization of the dream would hit him like a hammer and he was devastated when he discovered all over again that they were still lost.

He got to his feet and rubbed his eyes. It was time to head up to his bed. He pulled on the shutters at the windows and blew out the candle stubs that were glowing at the tableside. He took a long weary look at the slashed drawing of Toad that still hung on the wall and then he took a last look out of the window before he climbed the stairs.

Did he really see what he thought he could see? Was that the black pumpkin rolling past or was he still seeing things? It was late, even for Jarvis. Sam had a score to settle. His anger rose up inside of him. He pulled on his boots and coat and stepped out into the snow, emerging quickly from the door and taking after the trundling wheels of the carriage.

'Jarvis, I want words with you. Jarvis!' But his cries went unheard and he struggled to keep up as the carriage grew smaller and smaller. He began to pant and puff, and was quickly out of breath. He couldn't keep going like he used to. He was angry and worn out all at the same time.

'I just want my boy!' he said to himself and he fell to his knees in the snow and covered his face with his hands as tears ran down his reddened cheeks. 'I just want my boy!'

'Come on, Sam. It's late,' came a voice. It was Mr and Mrs Beetry from the candle store. Mr Beetry put his arms around Sam and pulled him to his feet, dusting him down to shake off the snow.

'Time for bed, you daft old beggar,' he said. 'Don't let this place get the better of you. He'll be fine, your boy. He ain't no fool.'

Mrs Beetry gave him a hug and wiped his cheeks with her apron.

'I know, I know. You're right,' said Sam, coming to his senses. 'I just miss him, that's all. I miss him badly.' And they helped him inside.

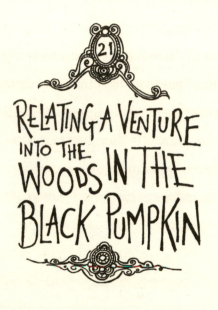

RELATING A VENTURE INTO THE WOODS IN THE BLACK PUMPKIN

Something flew overhead. It appeared like a small flock of witches clumped together. All Pip could do was stay calm and carry on. He steered the carriage into a bend to avoid them. There was a bridge up ahead and its archway formed a tunnel under which he could conceal himself for a brief moment. Had they seen him? Perhaps they had, perhaps they hadn't. He waited a moment as they passed over and headed for the forest. The children hoped to avoid as much contact as possible. They knew Jarvis was an old misery, so as long as Pip kept his head down and didn't say much they would be in character.

The three of them felt the forest looming. Toad poked his head out from the cloak and called out to Pip, 'Keep calm, brother. You're doing an excellent job.'

A shiver ran down Pip's spine. But it was not a feeling of fear – quite the opposite. It was the feeling he'd had when Toad called him 'brother'. It seemed to give him confidence in his task and buoyed up his spirits.

They grew nervous and held on tight. Not far to go before they were in the thick of those woods. They could hear the swishing and bowing of the branches now. A stiff breeze was swaying the frailest of the brushwood.

A clattering walkway of wooden panels announced the timber bridge that crossed into the leafy suburbs of the Hollow as the wheels rolled across them. There was less snow here and the ride became bumpier. Stiff roots

tried their best to upturn the rickety black pumpkin.

Spindly woody fingers scratched the roof of the mobile prison as if to try and tear open the insides and pull out prisoners. Pip knew the woods would be against them. There was something about those trees he knew not to trust and they seemed to know more than you would give credit to a tree.

Howling and barking began to circle the woods. Strange night noises resounded from trunk to trunk like echoes bouncing across the landscape. Pip ran his hand over his belt where Captain Dooley was tied. Perhaps it was a mistake bringing him back into the forest, but he had not wanted to lose sight of him. He mustn't let go of him, whatever happened.

And then to Pip's surprise a nearby crow landed on his shoulder. 'Shall I steer you to the keep, sire. Esther does not seem to be here. It is dark and I know your eyes will not be as good as mine.'

Pip's heart leapt and he was sure it could be heard thumping. He tried to settle himself. He didn't answer. He simply nodded and hoped the crow would not push him for an answer.

'Straight on and mind the low branches,' she said.

Toad watched her from beneath. He felt she'd taken a sneaky look down at him but he could not be sure. It was darker than he could have imagined and his eyes were still adjusting.

'Straight ahead, sire, and pull to the left in the clearing. There is a steep dip, so do hold on.'

Again Pip nodded but as the carriage dropped down, the hood of the cloak slipped and his hand was quick to pull it back across. Perhaps she hadn't noticed in the darkness.

Something ran at the side of the black pumpkin, clawing its hands on the doors and peering in. Heavy, hot breath poured in through the barred window and yellowy eyes spied their victims.

'Down, Fenris,' pleaded the crow. 'You will see them eventually.'

'The undergate is just ahead. Are you heading to the keep, sire?' it questioned.

Again Pip nodded. All three of them grew more nervous, their hearts beating in unison. This was it.

She steered them forward through the dark and a

chink of orange light turned out to be fire beacons burning at the mouth of the undergate.

'You'll find your way from here, sire,' she said and she lifted from his shoulders, disappearing into the dark of night.

They were alone now except that howls and squawks from the woods surrounded them. The carriage dropped into a low spiralling descent, gradually becoming steeper. More torches lit the way and Pip could see the walls of the labyrinth at close hand now, and the claw marks decorating the walls.

'Look!' he said. 'It's OK, you can see. There's no one here. Take a peek.' And their heads came out briefly for a moment.

It was quiet. It seemed there really was no one else here. It was a dark, dank ominous-looking hole.

Soon they would be rescuing the children that were harboured in the keep. If they could escape the forest in the same way that they came in, the plan would be a simply executed success.

AT WHICH POINT THE LOST CHILDREN ARE FOUND

The black pumpkin was spiralling towards the end of the undergate tunnel and the gnarled and woody entrance to the keep. It was stony silent but Pip and the others knew that for sure, up ahead, was a prison already filling up with the children of Hangman's Hollow.

Pip watched with dread as the root-riddled walls began to move. There were things attached to those tunnelled dug-outs. Creatures that had not been apparent at first sight, moving, slowly, awakening to the rumble of Jarvis's carriage. Something hung down from above with staring eyes. Pip averted his gaze and tried his best to appear unmoved by what was around him.

Unexpectedly, out from the darkness appeared the dreadful figure of Roach. His four arms poking out from his jacket. His strange glare, one dark eye and one milky white. He was a terrifying sight. He held a torch aloft and his wizened figure became apparent, all spindly and tall, an insectoid in a bedraggled ill-fitting outfit. Pip had seen Roach when first escaping from the forest, but only at a great distance. It was quite a shock to see him up close and he had a real task just to cover up his shock and fright. Pip bowed his head as if to acknowledge the man and conceal himself at the same time.

Roach beckoned him onwards, waving his

hand. He squinted into the porthole of the carriage as they passed through. Hopefully it was too dark for him to see that they didn't carry any prisoners.

Up ahead was a further gateway, more like a door, constructed from steel and wood, with a small barred opening in the centre. Someone or something stood at the entrance. It was small and goblin-like, hunched and skinny with pale skin and lank hair. It held a lantern and as they drew close it inserted the keys into the lock.

'Dis way, Misser Jarvis.'

It pushed open the keep door and they moved on. The little fellow peered into the carriage as they passed. He held his lantern aloft as he gazed inside.

'Why you don't got nuffink in der, Misser Jarvis?'

Pip pretended he hadn't heard the gatekeeper and carried on moving.

'Jus you tells Bodkin when you's ready to come out, Misser Jarvis, sir,' said the strange little man and he handed over his burning torch to what he thought was the city warden .

'Anyfink else you wants, Misser Jarvis, you jus calls Bodkin.'

'Bodkin!' exclaimed Toad quietly beneath his cloak. 'Strange name for a … whatever it was!'

'Shhh,' urged Frankie.

In they went, the carriage rolling slowly over the undulations of the root-bound earth, and as they passed into the cave the faces of small children began to show around them. They scattered into the corners like rabbits frightened by the sight of foxes. Whenever Jarvis returned, they knew they should hide. Most of them had felt the tip of his shiny hook at some point and some had scars to prove it. He would not hesitate to lash out if he felt the need.

They pulled the cloak away and revealed themselves. 'It's all right, it's me, Toad from the tavern.'

'And Pip,' said Pip.

'And Frankie Duprie, from the bakery.'

'Mister Jarvis isn't here. He's locked up in the city prison. We came in disguise. The woodsfolk thought we were him,' explained Toad in a loud whisper. 'We come to get you out. We need you.'

To begin with there was no response, but then slowly the children emerged from their holes. First their faces appeared, the lantern light reflecting in their pupils. Then their bedraggled figures materialized, their clothes tattered and worn and their bodies bony and waisted.

'They'll be hungry. I never thought to bring food,' said Pip.

'I've got bread,' said Frankie, taking a parcel from her apron pocket, 'I've always got bread. You should know that.' She smiled and then she handed it among the children. They pinched it from her and scuttled back as if still frightened.

Pip held the lantern to them so that Toad might know some of their faces. There were some he knew and some he didn't. Young McCreedy, the Brice boy, the Carraway twins. Mrs Malvern's daughters. They must have been here for some time. They looked different – older, definitely, and taller. He counted the children. There were twelve. It would be a squeeze to get them in the carriage and they would have to endure the onlookers peering in. It would look suspicious, taking children out from the keep!

'I have an idea,' said Pip. 'It could work.'

'Not again!' said Frankie. She could not help but despair at the boys' wild ideas. So far they had already cajoled her into far more than she would have liked to have been involved in.

But within minutes they were bundling the children into the confines of the black pumpkin. There were seats on either side. No use of course, but they lifted up to reveal neat little cubby holes. Pip had remembered the way that Toad had described the carriage after taking his first journey. Two either side would hide four of them. If three had the strength to cling on they could fit side by side beneath the carriage, holding on to the axle. Three could lie in the floor space, and two more in the footwell with the surplus of the cloak draped over them. That was twelve, plus the three disguised as Jarvis made fifteen children in total.

It was worth a try. And after all, there was little choice.

WHEN IT SEEMS THAT BODKIN IS CONFUSED

After much shuffling and squeezing into small spaces, the crew of children were ready to make their journey. Like a crew of hidden pirates they were about to set sail secretly aboard their black ship. The pumpkin turned itself around in the squat space of the forest keep. Pip could feel the carriage struggling with its newly acquired weight. It strained itself to make the turn, the horse braying as she found herself pulling much harder, the roof scraping against the earthen ceiling. But they would, all of them, soon be glad to be out of the forest prison.

Pip rapped on the door and waited. Bodkin's pointy little head showed itself, yellowy eyes squinted through the barred window of the door and then he disappeared again. They waited a moment longer until they heard the chink of keys and the turn of the lock in its barrel. Then the door opened with a distinct creak and light spilled inwards from the torchlit labyrinth of tunnels ahead.

Pip pulled on the reins and grunted his best impression of Jarvis's grumbling tones, handing the flaming torch back to the strange figure of Bodkin.

'Fankin you kindly, Misser Jarvis, sir. Master

Bodkin at your service,' he said all at once and then he made a small bow and grinned with pointed teeth.

They moved on quickly, eager to escape interrogation. Still there were creatures meandering about the labyrinth beyond the keep. Pip kept his head down. Only moments to go before they were free and making their way through the frozen trees and undergrowth. At this moment he longed for the freedom of the forest. Where before it had seemed like a foreboding place, now it smelled of freedom. If they got that far, they would feel as if they had made their escape.

The carriage was winding upwards. The return was uphill and it felt like a struggle. Pip urged the horse onwards but he could see the sweat forming on her back and the steam clouding around her nostrils as she pulled ahead. The wheels were slipping in the dirt but eventually a grip was regained and they were off again.

'Come on, old girl,' he whispered to her as they went. For a short while it levelled out and she could take a breath or two. Pip had no idea how the children were coping. It was the ones beneath the axle that were the biggest worry. If they couldn't hold on, they would fall into the path of the carriage and be seen.

Bodkin was still poised at the door to the keep. He had turned the lock and placed the key back on his belt. But something was bothering him a great deal. He was scratching his head and trying to work something out and no matter how he tried to reason with the problem in his head, it definitely made no sense. 'No sense at all,' he said to himself.

Again, creatures clambered around the walls as the carriage passed. Leering into the space and searching with their yellowy eyes through the portholes. Something climbed right on to the top of the roof as they went. Pip tried not to look around but Toad was pulling on his legs and whispering to him to take a look at what made the clatter. Inside the children tried to remain calm but the scraping sound of claws on the roof brought great concern. If it decided to climb inside they would have problems.

'What is it?' whispered Frankie. 'I can't see.'

'Dunno,' said Toad. 'Tell you in a minute when it climbs on top of us.'

'Stop it!' said Frankie.

Up ahead, the tunnel ceiling came closer to the carriage roof and the thing attached itself to a wall space to clear the narrowing gap. Its claws dug into the woody roots that wormed their way down and the creature rested itself in a small hole. Pip wiped the sweat from his brow and braced himself for another climb.

Still, Bodkin was troubled. 'Erm … umm … no … hmmmmm!' He scratched his pointy head and closed one eye. He stared upwards, as if perhaps the answer floated around over his head, but no, he still couldn't see it. 'Hmmmmmm … erm … no. Bodkin still muddled!'

The Malvern girls and the Brice boy were now hanging on desperately. All the strength was being sapped from their arms as they gripped the rear axle and kept their feet hoisted on to the front. Pip had told them that as soon as they cleared the labyrinth and emerged into the woods, they could take a moment to stop and then they could climb inside the carriage. But for the moment, they must suffer.

Edgar McCreedy lay curled up inside the cubby hole beneath the rear seat. One of the Carraway twins squeezed in alongside him. Edgar shook with fright. Soon he would be back with his parents but he had promised himself he would not open his eyes again until he heard his mother's voice.

Toad sneaked a look from his position under the cloak and passed word to Frankie, who was unable to see. 'Nearly there. I can see the torchlight at the undergate. Fingers crossed.'

Only Fenris guarded the exit. He wandered across in

front of the carriage and, using his long snout, he sniffed nosily at its base, raising a growl as he came. The smell of children had become a familiar scent upon it but still it made him bare his teeth. Pip pushed past, urging the carriage wheels onwards as the wolf stepped back.

They were clear. The view of the snow-covered ground was a welcome sight, signalling their escape. A refreshing brisk wind whirled around them. Pip carried on and waited until the light from the undergate had disappeared and then he stopped to let the others climb inside. The discomfort of the footwell and the pain endured while attached to the axle was replaced by the relative ease and comfort of the hard seats in the carriage.

They looked from the rounded portholes in the doors as they rumbled over the roots and through the snowy forest. Light from the city was beginning to show itself as a vague orangey glow through the silhouetted skeletons of the winter trees.

Home was in sight.

WHERE WE DISCOVER WHAT IS TROUBLING BODKIN

Roach was watching Bodkin scratch his head and quizzing himself over something. He fiddled with the keys at his waist and was staring upwards with a twisted expression fixed on his face.

'Is there something bothering you, Bodkin?'

'Oh, its nuffink, Misser Roach.'

144

'No, do tell me, Bodkin. What on earth is troubling that pointy little head of yours?'

Bodkin turned to Roach and fixed his troubled gaze on him. 'Well … da fing is, Misser Roach … beggin yer pardon me askin, but, when did Misser Jarvis fix 'is 'and?'

'When did … Mister Jarvis … fix his hand?'

'Yes, sir! When did Misser Jarvis fix 'is 'and?'

'Bodkin, I have no idea what you are talking about, but please do explain.'

'Oh, it dunt matter. Bodkin gets easily muddled,' said the strange little figure and he stared downwards at the floor, as if embarrassed by his own stupidity.

'Please …' urged Roach, 'carry on.'

'Well, sir, yer see, when Misser Jarvis give me da torchlight back he had two 'ands, sir. One 'and was takin' der reigns, sir … and (he paused to think a moment)…'

'Yes, Bodkin, do go on, I'm intrigued,' said Roach as a realization began to dawn over him.

'And … da uvver one pass me da torch. Misser Jarvis not got two 'ands, sir. Misser Jarvis got one 'and on der right and a 'ook on da left!'

Roach closed his eyes as he took a large intake of air in through his nose and then heaved a great big sigh.

'Whassa matter, Misser Roach. You no look too well.'

'We've been double-crossed, Bodkin. Bring the dogs. Call the bark demons and tell the others to gather at the undergate. And hurry. We won't be foiled again.'

'Yessir, Misser Roach,' said Bodkin and he hobbled off at high speed, waving his torch as he went and calling out at the top of his voice. 'We's been double-crossed.' And as he ran, he wondered what on earth being double-crossed was, and why it had made Mister Roach so angry. But Bodkin suspected he was probably muddled again and so he thought nothing of it, and of course, he wouldn't ask another stupid question.

In less than no time at all, the foresters were gathered, howling and whooping at the undergate, waiting for the signal to head out and begin the short hunt. The herd of cackling and cawing beasts were thundering in a swift procession towards the black pumpkin.

A flock of witches stayed behind. They had other methods. They were assembled, all of them, around a small fire. Hogwick spoke up, whispering strange words and calling up the curse of the Spindlewood forest to work its magic.

Pip and his companions were ambling along nicely into the snowy depths of the forest, the wheels rolling comfortably across the ground.

'We did it,' said Toad, poking his head out from beneath the cloak and wearing his best grin.

And then Frankie popped out. 'Well done, boys,' she said. She had been surprised at her own bravery.

A distant assembly of cries interrupted their mood. They had begun to grow almost relaxed, knowing that they were reaching the safety of the city. But the noise that came from behind them stirred them into anxiety.

'What's that?' asked Pip.

'Some kind of excitement among the woodsfolk, Pip. You'd best step up the pace,' said Toad.

Frankie and Toad had emerged and were sat alongside Pip at the front, the cover pulled across them to shut out the worst of the weather. Frankie stood up and looked back over the top of the pumpkin. Something moved in the distance – shapes swiftly passing between the trees. Pip pulled on the reigns but they were without torchlight and the journey was much harder at a swifter pace. The wheels were slipping as they sped up over the packed snowy ground and they shifted from side to side as they steered between the trees. Pip could feel the weight too. It made it twice as difficult to drive the carriage.

Somewhere nearby the trees began to stir. Something shifted in their make up – a stirring that came from the tips of the roots and filled the whole of the trunk and branches. It was as if they had come to life. The desire to move and flex their long limbs stirred around in their woody souls.

Distraction came to the children in the form of whooping and hollering, howling and squawking. Something flew parallel to the carriage in the distance, darting, batlike between the uprights. Pip looked to his left and then to his right. The twilight seekers were on them and very quickly, they were surrounded.

Crunch. The carriage had hurled itself into a dip and was almost turned on its side, its front end speared into the ground. The back wheels were in the air and spun, slower and slower until they too came to a stop. The horse was still attached to the carriage and scrambled with its front legs as if to climb from the dip, but there was no way it would release itself. If Pip could have freed it, he could have used it to flee the forest, but it would take too much time to dismantle the frame. They had to leave her there in the ditch, struggling to get back on to her feet.

'Quick,' said Frankie. 'On foot, we can make it to the city.'

They hurriedly pulled the others out from inside the carriage. The door was jammed and so their skinny figures were yanked out through the porthole window like stubborn weeds pulled from the ground.

Together they stumbled through the forest. They ran and ran and ran, their breath heaving, their hearts thumping. It seemed like perhaps they were far enough ahead to make it. Were they being too hopeful? Time would tell.

Hogwick's curse began to stir. The roots of the Spindlewood trees squirmed upon the ground like worms. Their snow-covered tendrils emerged like spring buds and then, as if life poured into them, they began whipping and winding. The lofty branches felt the same ripple of movement. The soft breezy waft of their limbs became a powerful, full-blooded swing.

Crack! Pip was clutched around the waist by the grip of a low-lying branch. *Whip!* Toad and Frankie were snatched by the vicious roots from the same tree. Birds lifted from the branches as they took on their own life and grabbed at the little ones. The others were subject to the same fate, almost as if the forest itself had turned on them. The McCreedy boy screamed. He was wick and almost got away. But the trees seemed to move in on him and blocked his path, sending him this way and that,

until finally, he fell to his knees in exhaustion. Mister Brice's boy was held aloft, tied with lashings of spindly branch wood. And then much the same became of the others. The forest tied itself around the children until they remained suspended against the trees, waiting for their captors to arrive and return them to their prison.

The foresters came to find the children waiting for them, like flies trapped in the webs of spiders, held still by the full and frightening force of the Spindlewood Forest.

With the carriage pulled out from the ditch the creatures howled excitedly as the children were released from the trees and pushed inside. The horse was steadied on her legs by Roach and adjusted back into her frame. She brayed awkwardly and stamped her hooves into the snow, breathing clouds of hot air.

'Steady, girl,' said Roach as he used his four arms to nurse her.

Something clawed its way on to the roof and settled into position, ready to alert the flock to any movement from within. Small bark demons hung at the portholes on the doors and peered menacingly at the screaming children. A flock of crows hovered overhead like a cloud of black rain waiting to descend. And the carriage was herded back towards the undergate by screaming, hysterical woodsfolk while the children awaited their fate.

AT WHICH POINT AN OPPORTUNITY PRESENTS ITSELF

Pip didn't think that he had ever been more frightened. He could barely make out the faces of the others but they were shoved in tight together. Toad was next to him and he could hear Frankie reassuring the young McCreedy boy.

Faces peered inside the black pumpkin. Beaked and long-snouted, they poked their excited heads into the portholes. And as they did, they squawked and squealed and argued amongst themselves while trying to take the best view. Their clawed hands and feet clamped themselves inside the window, scraping and scratching at the panels of the carriage.

Pip's heart was beating furiously. Toad seemed to have no fear. He edged towards one of the windows and began to lash out at the woodsfolk. 'Let us out, you freaks!' he called, bashing at their clawed hands as they edged inside.

Torches shone in the darkness of the woods. They must be back at the undergate. But no, the children could sense that outside the animals had become quiet. They were puzzled at the lights ahead.

Voices came – distant inaudible voices, shouts and hollering that seemed like they came out of anger. The carriage had slowed to a halt now and the woodsfolk stood silently watching as the bedlam approached. A group were visible. They held flaming torches aloft. Some were on horseback and some on foot. But someone ran ahead of them and he had almost reached the woodsfolk when he began shouting. His cloak flapped in the wind and as he drew close to the orange light his hook could be seen glinting in the darkness.

'Draw your weapons, you fools, and be ready for battle. City folk approaching.'

At this, Pip's heart thumped harder. It was Jarvis, with Esther flying on behind. Escaped from his hole with the city following in pursuit. War was about to be waged on forest turf. In a breath, the plight of the prisoners had been forgotten. The bark demons howled out for support and the air grew blacker still with flocking witches. Panic broke among the four-legged ones and the gathering of weapons ensued.

Pip called to his brethren through the noise and darkness. 'This is our chance. Stick together and keep going.' And with that, he pushed down gently on the door handle and led the others to safety while the distraction allowed him the opportunity.

The whole earth seemed to shake as horses thundered towards the foresters. The shouting grew louder and the howls of the forest pierced the night air like sirens.

'And where do you think you're going?' came a

voice. But whatever it was received his answer in the form of a branch across the back of the head as Toad delivered a blow from behind.

'Come on,' said Toad, 'we need to move quickly.'

A herd of lost children made haste across the forest floor. The only sound for now was the breathless gasping and heavy breathing coming from their mouths. That and the crisp crunch of the snowy surface breaking beneath their feet, twigs and branches snapping beneath them. They were running hard and their trail could be picked out by the puffs of foggy breath and a peppering of footprints in the icy white ground.

They did not know where they would head. Only that they should escape while the fighting between city and forest continued and the distraction was enough to allow their getaway.

In the distance makeshift weapons clashed and blood spilled across the clear white of the forest floor. Screams of pain and effort echoed between the uprights of the trees. Blades and shields crashed against the woody bark and the cries of the forest cut the stillness

of the air in two. Horses reared upwards on to their back legs.

Still the children kept on running. They helped each other along, pulling at one another's tunics and cloaks. Soon they would break out into the city and, although they had no idea where they would head, freedom beckoned them onwards.

They felt the surface of wooden boards beneath their feet. They were crossing the gateway to the city streets and as they reached the other side of the bridge, instinctively they stopped and took deep, heavy breaths. They were a big group now and it would prove difficult to hide.

Even here in the streets the clash of city and forest could be heard. Roars and screams and shouts of war, piercing the night. A low rumble of disturbance filtered between the trees.

'Where now?' said Pip, looking expectantly at Toad.

'Somewhere that can take the lot of us,' he replied, gasping and wheezing and looking around him. Were they still all here?

Frankie began to count and her finger worked its

way around the group.
'Fifteen,' she said. 'All present
and correct.'

And so they kept on
running. They still had no idea
where they were heading but
they kept on all the same, with
their hearts pounding and their
cold breath clouding around
them. They were weak, all of
them, and they would have to
find somewhere soon or else
the smallest ones might drop
to their knees and fall flat
in the snow.

'Not much further,'
encouraged Toad but in truth,
he did not know where they
might go.

WHEN SOMEONE UNEXPECTED RETURNS TO THE WOODS

In typical Jarvis style he had avoided the confrontation in the forest. He was a true coward. The clash of steel and drawing of blood was down to his escape from the city, but he had been the only one to sit out on the fight. It was a grim and gruesome affair. These things always were. There were, as expected, casualties on both sides and the forest was littered with the remains of a fight. Broken weapons, injured men and horses and other sights best left to the imagination. The city folk had returned empty-handed, their prisoner lost in the onslaught.

It was much later when the man Jarvis stepped out from the hollow of a tree. The battle was long finished and all was still and silent.

His feet crunched on the hardened white surface. The first hint of daylight was pushing the darkness back into its hole and Esther steered one eye downwards as he emerged. She had faithfully waited by his side.

He dusted himself down, took a long, snake-eyed stare about himself and then he began to walk back to the undergate. And as he walked he dreamed himself a story, of how he had fought for his life against the city folk. He thought so long and hard of the tale that he almost began to believe it himself.

The witches were circling above. Darting between the forest and the city, searching for the little ones through the air with their black shadows dashing across the rooftops like scurrying rats. The children moved quickly in the safety of the shaded corners of the streets and houses.

'Stop,' said Frankie, calling out to Toad at the front.

'What is it?'

'The Duprie bakery is near. We should head inside. We can use the ovens and make bread. We can keep warm. It's empty and for now, it's safe.'

And so they all turned and followed Frankie. Like marching ants they changed direction and snaked in a line through the alleyways.

When they reached the bakery it was boarded over. Snow piled high against the walls and it had

remained untouched for some time. A sadness overwhelmed Frankie, bringing tears flooding down her face. She had pictured it with its warm fireside glow through the window, the snow twinkling in the soft orange light and her parents standing in the shop front. But it was dark and empty. Paint peeled itself from the doorway and the old sign creaked rustily on its hinges in the breeze.

Pip stepped in. 'We have to be careful. It's undisturbed. If we break in, we leave a mark.'

'Around the back,' said Frankie, wiping her tears, and she showed them the cellar door which lay flat upon the cobbles. Carefully they raised it upwards and allowed the children to file inside. Pip came last, dispersing footprints with a discarded broom and letting down the hatch gently.

Frankie set about lighting the ovens in the basement. They were vented into the sewer outlets and so they need not worry about the smoke piping up and announcing their position.

A whooshing sweeping sound filtered through the alleyways. The last of the twilight seekers were giving up the search for the little ones. It would grow light soon and they should be back in their holes. Jarvis was holding court around a fire in the forest. He feigned an injury and told his tale. Of how he had taken on Hector Stubbs, the city mayor, and wounded him, maybe even fatally. And how soon he would take his position when the whole forest rose up in arms against the authorities. They must be ready for war, he had announced. And soon.

WHEN AT LAST, THE SURPRISE ENDING IS DELIVERED

It was late now but the children were all settled into their corners and huddled together like baby mice, taking comfort from each other and burying their faces into their chests. The heat from the oven was becoming blissfully warm. There were sacks of flour stacked in one corner, enough to keep them going for some time.

'I can feel my toes again,' said young Edgar, rubbing his feet and hands.

'Come closer to the ovens,' said Frankie and she herded them nearer to the heat.

In the morning she would show them how to make bread and they could feed themselves until they felt strong enough to move on. They were not sure yet just what they would do. Perhaps they should leave the city for good, some had suggested, and make their way across the ice valley. Or find the others across the city, in basements and attic spaces, in groups or alone.

'We should build an army and take the forest and return triumphant to the city, never again to be ignored,' said Pip, and Toad cheered in agreement. But now was not the time to decide. Rest and a good feed in the morning. That was their first task.

Pip watched the others drift into sleep. Toad was out like a light, face first into the sack of flour he lay upon. Frankie was drifting off. She gazed over at him and smiled but she was too tired to speak.

Soon Pip was the only one awake. He knew they

were safe and he felt good for now. Rescuing the others had been a triumph but he was exhausted. He eased himself into comfort, but something pressed into his side. It was a small hessian bag. Of course, it was the Captain. He had quite forgotten that they had brought him along, and Pip suddenly felt uneasy that they had a traitor in the camp. Perhaps he should throw him into the oven and have done with it. He was far too dangerous. They didn't need him to find the others.

'Go on, Pip, do it,' he heard himself saying. 'Burn him. He's only a doll.'

He grew nervous. He had never held him in his hand before. He pulled the drawstring at the top of the bag and felt a shuffle of movement inside. The feather in Captain Dooley's hat sprang up and Pip grabbed his hat and eeked him out of the bag.

And he would have thrown him straight into the oven. Really, he would. But the wooden doll felt the hand around him as Pip took him by the waist. And something came into the Captain's thoughts.

'Master Pipkin,' he squeaked at last. 'One half of the Pipkin two. Born of the same hour and separated at birth. Left alone in the orphanage without the love of his brother. Poor old Eddie Pipkin.' And then just as quickly as he had awoken he fell back to sleep.

Pip's eyes grew wider and his heart beat so fast that he could hear it thumping through his chest. He wanted to waken everyone. To scream out loud to Frankie. Was it really the truth? Did he have a brother? Was that the missing part of him that kept him awake all night? And where on earth could he be?

How could he not share his news? He rose up and crossed the room to where Frankie lay and she woke to see him smiling.

'Frankie, listen. The Captain has spoken. I have a brother. A real brother. I'm a twin.'

But she was so tired that she thought she was dreaming and she drifted back into a heavy sleep. Pip looked around him. They were away, all of them. Blissfully drifting in the warmth of the bakery. He should let them rest, of course he should.

And so Pip lay there in the dark hours, bewildered and excited, until he was overcome with tiredness. As the light from the fire died he felt himself slipping helplessly into sleep, and dreamed of what was to come.

Join Pip in the final showdown between forest and city ...

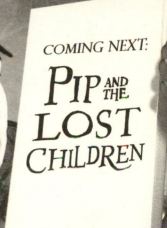

COMING NEXT:

PIP AND THE LOST CHILDREN

Written and illustrated by
CHRIS MOULD

978 0 340 97071 3   £4.99 pb

Chris Mould

Chris Mould went to art school at the age
of sixteen. During this time, he did various
jobs, from delivering papers to washing-up
and cooking in a kitchen. He has won the
Nottingham Children's Book Award and
been commended for the Sheffield. He
loves his work and likes to write and draw
the kind of books that he would have liked
to have on his shelf as a boy. He is married
with two children and lives in Yorkshire.

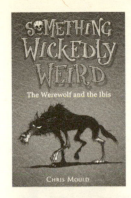

SOMETHING WICKEDLY WEIRD
The Werewolf and the Ibis
CHRIS MOULD

SOMETHING WICKEDLY WEIRD
The Ice Pirates
CHRIS MOULD

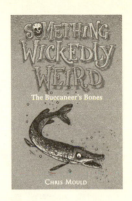

SOMETHING WICKEDLY WEIRD
The Buccaneer's Bones
CHRIS MOULD

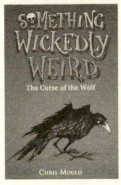

SOMETHING WICKEDLY WEIRD
The Curse of the Wolf
CHRIS MOULD

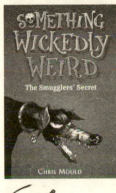

SOMETHING WICKEDLY WEIRD
The Smugglers' Secret
CHRIS MOULD

SOMETHING WICKEDLY WEIRD
The Golden Labyrinth
CHRIS MOULD

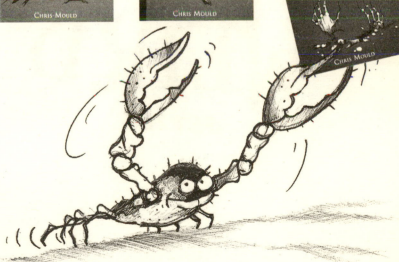

Praise for the

SOMETHING
WICKEDLY
WEIRD

series:

'Engagingly illustrated ...
cheerful, fast-moving romp.'

Carousel

'From the moment they claw their
way out of a graveyard you know
you are onto a winner.'

Publishing News

'A riveting read for newly
independent readers.'

Bookfest

'A splendid mix of Gothic horror
and cartoon-style fun.'

Bookbag

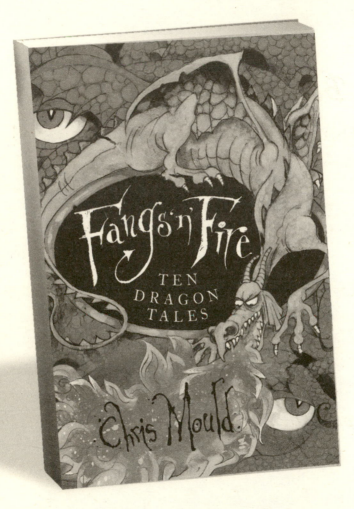

978 0 340 94476 9 £5.99 pb

Beware the dragon ...

This book of fiery dragon tales is adapted,
written and superbly illustrated
by award-winner

Chris Mould

A wonderful collection packed full of fangs
and fire, dragon myths and legends:
from *George and the Dragon* to the
Chinese myth *The Eyeless Dragons*

Open this book at your own peril ...